"These attacks could all be aimed at me.

"He could be trying to throw you at me as a distraction."

"If so, it's working," Adalyn muttered. "We're both distracted, and that's not going to get better."

Nolan had to agree. In fact, it was probably going to get a whole lot worse. There were so many ways the Grave Digger could come at them. And judging from the stark look in Adalyn's eyes, she was as well aware of that as he was.

Sighing, he reached out and pulled her into his arms for a hug. Yeah, it was a mistake. He was good at making those when it came to Adalyn, but damn it all to hell, he just needed her right now. Needed to feel her close to him like this. Needed the reminder they were both alive.

She looked up at him, and Nolan made another mistake.

He dipped down his head and touched his mouth to hers.

SPURRED TO JUSTICE

USA TODAY Bestselling Author

DELORES FOSSEN

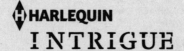

HARLEQUIN
INTRIGUE

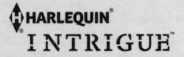

Recycling programs
for this product may
not exist in your area.

ISBN-13: 978-1-335-58240-9

Spurred to Justice

Harlequin Enterprises ULC
22 Adelaide St. West, 41st Floor
Toronto, Ontario M5H 4E3, Canada
www.Harlequin.com

Printed in U.S.A.

Delores Fossen, a *USA TODAY* bestselling author, has written over one hundred novels, with millions of copies of her books in print worldwide. She's received a Booksellers' Best Award and an RT Reviewers' Choice Best Book Award. She was also a finalist for a prestigious RITA® Award. You can contact the author through her website at www.deloresfossen.com.

Books by Delores Fossen

Harlequin Intrigue

The Law in Lubbock County

Sheriff in the Saddle
Maverick Justice
Lawman to the Core
Spurred to Justice

Mercy Ridge Lawmen

Her Child to Protect
Safeguarding the Surrogate
Targeting the Deputy
Pursued by the Sheriff

Visit the Author Profile page at Harlequin.com.

CAST OF CHARACTERS

FBI agent Nolan Dalton—While on the hunt for a notorious serial killer, he's reunited with his ex, who's the killer's latest target.

Adalyn Baxter—A troubled former cop who doesn't like relying on anyone to keep her safe, but she's forced to team up with Nolan to stop more murders, including their own.

FBI agent Cody Hill—Nolan's partner, who could have secrets and info linked to the serial killer whom the press has dubbed the Grave Digger.

Sheriff Jeb Mercer—Decades ago, someone kidnapped this now-retired sheriff's toddler son, and that kidnapping could be linked to the murders that are happening now.

Donny Ray Carver—He's on death row for murdering Nolan's father, but it's possible he's manipulating the Grave Digger from behind bars.

Russell Mason—Adalyn's strong-minded boss and the head of a security company. He could be the killer and using the tools of his trade to hide his crimes.

Jeremy Waite—He's Donny Ray's best friend, and he just might go to any lengths to do Donny Ray's bidding.

Chapter One

Seven minutes. FBI Agent Nolan Dalton knew that was all the time he had left. If he didn't get to her by then, she'd be dead.

Batting aside low-hanging tree limbs and hurdling over the underbrush, Nolan ran through the thick woods of the Texas Hill Country while he kept his right hand over the Glock in his holster. His heart was pounding. His breath came out in hard, sharp gusts. He didn't stop. Didn't steel himself up for the possibility of being gunned down. Nolan just ran as if a woman's life depended on it.

Because it did.

On the other side of him, his fellow agent, Cody Hill, kept up the breakneck pace. They sprinted along the trail—such that it was—following the drag marks and the trampled shrubs. Just as the killer had instructed them to do in the text that he'd sent Nolan.

Since Nolan had been an FBI agent for a little over seven years, he wasn't a fan of following a killer's orders, but he'd had no choice about it this time. Because this killer, the man that the news media had dubbed the Grave Digger, had said if Nolan got to the woman within an hour, she might still be alive.

Might.

But a chance of her surviving was better than nothing. Especially since Nolan didn't believe this was a hoax. The Grave Digger had convinced Nolan of that by including a photo of one of his previous victims in the text. A photo that only the Grave Digger himself or someone with him could have shot.

It'd taken fifty-three of those sixty minutes for Nolan and Cody just to get from their office in San Antonio to the Hill Country trail that the killer had mapped out for them. And they'd come alone. As the killer had ordered. The Grave Digger had made it clear that if they brought someone else with them, then the woman and anyone trying to save her would die.

Of course, the killer could be just stringing them along so he'd have easy targets to gun down, but Nolan had decided to go with his gut. His gut said, *Do as you're told and get to the woman now.* All the while taking what precautions he could, of course. That's why he had his gun ready.

Nolan didn't want to think of another woman dying, of how terrified she would be right now. It would only get in the way of his focus.

But he thought of her anyway.

Nolan didn't know the name of the gray-haired woman, but everything about her seemed to be screaming for help. Maybe literally screaming now, too, because if the Grave Digger stuck to pattern, he would have bound her hands and feet and buried her in a shallow hole that he then covered with enough thick debris that would insure she'd soon run out of oxygen.

Five minutes.

The seconds were ticking off in his head as they ran. Nolan knew that, like him, Cody was also trying to keep watch. Trying to make sure they weren't about to be ambushed.

Sweat slipped down Nolan's face and into his eyes, but he didn't take the time to wipe it away. The blistering Texas heat certainly wasn't giving them any breaks, but as bad as it was for Cody and him, it would be a million times worse for the woman.

"The clearing should be just ahead," Cody rattled off through his now thin breath.

Yeah, it should be. On the frantic drive over from San Antonio, both of them had memorized the map so they wouldn't have to stop and take a look at their phones to figure out where the heck they were going. If the killer hadn't given them bogus info, then they should see the spot in under a minute. Then, they'd find the woman fifteen feet on the east side of the open space.

Four minutes.

Nolan felt the jolt of relief when they finally reached the clearing. If this info was accurate, then maybe it would be true about the woman still being alive. He didn't hesitate to head to the east, and it was only a couple of seconds before they made it to the edge of another stretch of woods. And then they came to a dead stop.

Both of them drew their guns and took aim.

There was a woman all right, but she wasn't in the ground. Nor did she have gray hair. She was a brunette, and she was on her knees. She was frantically digging at a mound of dirt and leaves.

"Stop," Nolan growled out.

The brunette's head snapped up, her panicked gaze connecting with his, and Nolan cursed. So did Cody because they both knew her.

She was Adalyn Baxter.

Once she'd been a San Antonio cop. A good one, too. And she'd also spent some nights in Nolan's bed. But that felt like a lifetime ago. A lifetime that had come crashing down around him two years earlier. That's when his father had been gunned down at Adalyn's house while he'd been waiting for Nolan to show up for a meet-the-family dinner.

There'd been no dinner. Only a hail of bullets that a murder suspect, Donny Ray Carver, had meant for Adalyn. Donny Ray had wanted to get back at the cop who'd been within days of arresting him, but he'd killed an innocent man instead.

Nolan hadn't blamed Adalyn for the attack. Or rather he'd tried not to do that. But it was the unwanted, unspoken blame that had torn them apart. Because Adalyn had indeed put the weight of that attack on her shoulders, and it had led to her turning in her badge. Turning away from Nolan, too.

"Don't just stand there," Adalyn snapped. "Help me. She's suffocating. We've only got just a couple of minutes left to get her out."

He exchanged a glance with Cody, and Nolan didn't exactly see anything reassuring in Cody's eyes. "You think Adalyn's the killer?" Cody muttered.

Adalyn cursed. "I'm not." She'd obviously heard Cody's question just fine. "Now, help me before she dies."

Nolan hadn't thought for one second that Adalyn was a killer, but even if he had, he couldn't have just stood there. Not with a woman in the ground. A woman he could save. He hurried to Adalyn, dropping down on his knees across from her. Seconds later, Cody did the same.

"What are you doing here?" Nolan demanded. He began to dig as Adalyn was doing. So did Cody.

"I got a text from the Grave Digger," she answered without looking at either of them. "He told me where to park and what trail to take. He said where I'd find a woman he buried. We're in time. She'll still be alive," Adalyn added in a mutter like a hopeful prayer.

Her breath and voice were as ragged as his were, and the sweat on her face clued him in that Adalyn had also run to get here. Not from the same direction though as Cody and he had or Nolan would have seen her car. There'd been no other vehicles on the last mile of the rural road or any parked by the trail. So, maybe she'd gotten different instructions. Ones that had obviously led them to the same place. What Nolan didn't know was why the killer would have sent Adalyn a text.

And that was just the first of many questions.

Soon, he'd want to know lots of details about her

connection to this, but for now, he just kept on digging, slinging off the dirt and debris as fast as he could. They were a good six inches down in the ground when Nolan spotted the small container of oxygen. Moments later, he pushed away enough dirt to see the woman's hair.

Silver gray.

She wasn't moving, but Nolan didn't focus on that. Neither did Cody or Adalyn. It was Adalyn who raked the dirt away from the woman's face. Despite the oxygen mask that was covering her mouth, Nolan could still see enough of her to know that it was the same woman in the photo.

"Is she breathing?" Cody blurted out.

Nolan had no idea. It was possible the oxygen tank was already empty. Maybe it'd been empty for so long that she'd already suffocated, but he hoped that wasn't what had happened.

Nolan dragged the woman from the shallow grave, moving her to solid ground so he could check to see if she was breathing and start CPR. Adalyn was on the same page he was because she ripped away the oxygen mask and began the mouth-to-mouth while Nolan started the hand compressions on her chest. He also tried to pick through the woman's features to see if there was anything he recognized about her. He didn't.

She looked like someone's grandmother.

That was his first thought. She was in her late fifties, early sixties, and there wasn't a drop of color in her face. She was thin with a willowy build, and Nolan could feel her ribs beneath his palms. Could feel the tape, too. The killer who'd put her here had wrapped her with duct tape, securing her arms to her sides and binding her bare feet. The tape was wound from just below her breasts to her wrists and from her midcalves to her ankles. It was so tight that Nolan doubted she'd been able to do more than squirm.

If that.

The killer had drugged his other victims. Not enough to make them unconscious. No. The sick SOB had wanted them alert enough to know exactly what was happening to them. He'd wanted them to fight for that last breath while feeling just one thing. The terror when they realized they were dying.

"I'm calling for an ambulance," Cody relayed to them, whipping out his phone. He stood, stepping a few feet away from them. "It might take a while though to get all the way out here."

Yeah, it would. This burial site wasn't exactly on the beaten path so they were probably looking at a half hour at best. Way too long. If the woman stood a chance of surviving, it would have to come through the CPR, a reminder that caused Nolan to work even harder. He'd had training on how to do this, but the training hadn't prepared him for the fight he was having with his own sickening dread. Dread because no matter how hard he tried, it might not be enough.

"Keep watch," Nolan reminded him though Cody was no doubt already doing that. Because the killer could have eyes on them. Waiting to start taking shots at them. It wouldn't do them any good if they saved the woman only for all of them to be killed by some-one who obviously enjoyed playing sick games.

"Breathe," Adalyn pled in between the mouth-to-mouth attempts.

Nolan wasn't sure who was more surprised when the woman seemingly listened to Adalyn's plea. She rattled out a cough and then sucked in a gasping breath.

"She's alive," Adalyn muttered.

There was a mountain-size amount of relief in her voice as she slipped her hands behind the woman's head and lifted her. Nolan took advantage of the upright position to wipe away more of the dirt from her face and nose.

The woman continued to cough in between taking in more of those gulps of air, but with each gulp, Nolan could see some of the color return to her face. Only then did he allow himself just a moment to level out his own breathing. They'd done it. They'd gotten to her in time to save her. There wouldn't be another dead body to add to the Grave Digger's tally. The next step though would be for them to keep her alive.

"The ambulance should be here in about twenty minutes," Cody said, hurrying toward them. "An ERT and backup are on the way, too."

ERT was an FBI Evidence Response Team who would process the scene, and like backup, the team would be coming from the field office in San Antonio. That meant Cody and he would be out here for a while. Not that either of them wanted to go anywhere else until they'd garnered every bit of info they could get from both this woman and the scene itself.

Cody dropped down on his knees beside the woman and leaned in closer so they were face-to-face. "I'm Special Agent Hill with the FBI. Who are you?" he asked.

She tried to answer, but the coughing made it impossible for her to speak. There were no streams or springs nearby and apparently none of them had brought water with them so they just had to wait for her to work through it. While she did, Nolan made a sweeping glance around them to try to fix the scene into his mind.

Like the first part of the trail, there were footprints and drag marks here, too. Obviously Cody, Adalyn and he had contaminated possible evidence just by coming into the area, but they hadn't had much of a choice about that. Saving a life had to be their top priority, and by some miracle that priority had worked. The woman was definitely breathing now.

Like the other victims of the Grave Digger, she was wearing only a bra and panties, but if the pattern held, she wouldn't have been raped. In fact, there'd been no signs at all of sexual assault on the other women. Stripping them of their clothes was likely just a way of adding to their fear and letting them know they had zero control over the situation. The control was all in the hands of the one about to kill them.

"I don't have any gloves or an evidence bag for the tape," Adalyn said as she examined it.

Nolan made a quick sound of agreement. The tape

might be able to provide them with trace evidence or prints. *Might*. Of course, there'd been no such evidence left behind on the other women. Still, there was a chance that the killer had made a mistake this time.

"Who are you?" Cody repeated to the woman.

She blinked hard, and Nolan tried to brush away the dirt from her eyelids. "Caroline Edmondson," she finally managed to say.

The name meant nothing to Nolan, and when he looked at Adalyn to see if she knew her, she only shook her head. Cody added his own headshake as well.

"Who did this to you?" Cody continued. "Who hurt you?" He'd kept his voice calm and level. No sense of urgency or fear. It was a ploy that might work to keep the woman from panicking.

Caroline squeezed her eyes shut a moment, and her forehead bunched up as if she was trying to squeeze out the memories. Nolan was betting though that some of those memories were clouded in a haze of whatever drug was still in her system.

"Blindfold," she finally said. "He put a blindfold on me. I didn't see his face, and he used some kind of thing on his throat to make his voice sound funny, like a cartoon." She stopped and moaned out a sob. "I don't want to see his face or hear his voice. I don't want to be here. I need to go home."

Nolan didn't tell her the truth. That it might be a very long time before that happened. She would have to be examined at the hospital. Probably admitted, too, at least for observation even if there weren't any injuries. Then, she would be questioned by the FBI. And even after that, she'd likely be going to a safe house until they could determine if she was still a target. Nolan was betting that she was.

The Grave Digger might want to have another go at the sole survivor of his killing spree.

"I'll make some calls and see if I can find out who she is," Cody muttered, moving away from them again. "And I'll go ahead and get a field kit from the SUV. While I'm there, I can leave a copy of the map so the EMTs will know where to find us."

Good idea. Well, it was a good idea as long as Cody didn't get ambushed along the path. But the kit was a must because it contained the things they could use to free Caroline from the tape. The EMTs would also need that map.

"Be careful," Nolan warned him.

Cody gestured with a thumbs-up but was already making a call as he hurried back toward the road.

"Three hours," Caroline muttered, getting Nolan's attention. A raw sob tore from her throat. "He said that's how long I'd have to be in the ground before you would come to save me."

Nolan had no idea if that three hours was accurate. None of the other victims had lived to tell them how long they'd been buried alive. But it was a good sign that Caroline remembered what the killer had told her. Maybe that meant she'd remember other things that could lead to the FBI identifying him.

"Can you tell me what happened to you?" Nolan asked her. "Can you tell me how you got here?"

She opened her mouth but didn't speak. However, her breathing kicked up. So did the pulse on her throat. The panic started to overtake her again, and Nolan couldn't be sure, but he thought she was having a flashback.

"Don't leave me," Caroline begged, looking at Adalyn. "I can hear his voice. I can feel his hands on me. Please don't let him take me again."

Adalyn looked her straight in the eyes. "I won't, and I won't leave you."

The next breath that Caroline took seemed to be one of relief, and despite her bound hands, she managed to touch her fingers to Adalyn's. Until then, Nolan hadn't been thankful about Adalyn being there, but he wanted Caroline to have what comfort she could, and she seemed to trust Adalyn. Unfortunately, the touching could compromise evidence. He didn't stop it though because Adalyn's and his DNA were already all over the woman and the scene.

"Are you an FBI agent, too?" Caroline asked Adalyn. The panic was already easing up in her voice.

Nolan saw the flash of emotion in Adalyn's dark blue eyes. Bad emotion. No doubt because it made Adalyn remember that she'd once had a badge.

"No," Adalyn answered. "I work for a security company."

Nolan had known about her taking that job at Secure Point. The company provided everything from personalized security systems to bodyguards. Nolan had had a run-in with the owner, Russell Mason, who made a habit of bumping up against the lines of the law when it came to what he considered the best interest of his clients. However, despite that, Secure Point had a good enough reputation. Still, it was a major step down from being a decorated SAPD homicide detective.

Of course, for Adalyn anything would have been a step down since she'd always wanted to be a cop. She'd told him that often enough during pillow talk. Not just married to the badge but in love with it.

"Are you in pain?" Adalyn whispered to the woman.

Caroline shook her head, and with her breathing and pulse leveling out, her eyelids drifted back down. Maybe because of the drugs. Or the shock. Either way, Nolan was thankful for that, too, and he hoped if she drifted off, the nightmares wouldn't get to her.

He knew plenty about nightmares.

Adalyn did, too.

Bad blood often started with actual blood, and it certainly had with Adalyn and him. Nolan hated that he couldn't rid himself of the memories and nightmares about his father's murder, but for now he shoved all of that aside so he could talk to Adalyn.

"Why did the Grave Digger text you?" he demanded.

Adalyn's mouth tightened for a moment. "I don't have a clue. And no, he hasn't contacted me before today." She paused, and Nolan thought Adalyn might be having to push aside some memories as well. "He attached pictures. Of Caroline…and one of your father."

Everything inside him went still. "My father?" Nolan questioned.

"Yes. The pictures are on my phone," Adalyn went on after she'd cleared her throat, "but the FBI will want to take a hard look at the one of your dad because I'm pretty sure it was taken from San Antonio PD files. I know it wasn't one released to the public."

Nolan silently cursed again. So, the killer might have hacking skills. Or was maybe a cop. But why had the Grave Digger added his father and Adalyn into the mix of this buried victim? It was yet another question that Nolan couldn't answer, not yet anyway, but that would only make him look harder. He wanted to catch this SOB and put him away for the rest of his miserable life.

"Nolan," Adalyn said a moment later. The breath she took was thin and filled with nerves, and she didn't say anything else until Nolan's gaze was locked with hers. "I didn't have anything to do with this, and I really don't have a clue why the Grave Digger sent me that text."

"Nolan?" Caroline repeated. Her eyes flew open, and her attention zoomed right to him. "Are you Special Agent Nolan Dalton?"

Confused as to how she'd know his name, Nolan nodded and waited for Caroline to continue. It didn't take long. "The man who took me told me to give Special Agent Nolan Dalton a message," Caroline blurted out, her words running together. "He made me memorize it and said if I didn't tell you that he'd come back for me." She shuddered. "He said he'd kill me if I didn't tell you."

An icy knot tightened in Nolan's gut. "What are you supposed to tell me?"

Some of the fog was gone from Caroline's eyes, but there was now a fresh coating of fear. No, not just fear. Terror. "That you aren't who you think you are." She whispered the words like a secret. A really bad one.

Of all the things Nolan had thought she might say, that hadn't even been on his radar. "I'm not who I think I am?" he pressed.

Caroline's nod was fast and frantic. "That you aren't Bill Dalton's son. You were never his son. Someone gave you to Bill Dalton, but you were never his."

Nolan kept his attention latched to Caroline, but he leaned back, studying her face. "Of course, I'm his son. *Was* his son," Nolan amended.

"No," Caroline insisted. "He said you weren't. And I'm supposed to show you this." She uncurled her fingers on her left hand. Exposing her palm and the words that were written there in tiny print.

"Nolan, the lie you're living will kill you," the message said. He read it aloud, trying to process each word.

Nolan looked at Caroline, hoping that along with the terror he'd see some answers as to what that meant, but she only shook her head and opened her right hand. There was more written here in the same black marker.

"Blood doesn't lie," Nolan read, and below it was a name.

Hell.

What was going on? Because the name on her hand was none other than Donny Ray Carver, the man who'd murdered Nolan's father.

Chapter Two

Donny Ray Carver.

Adalyn had hoped she'd never hear that name again, especially since she heard it often enough in her nightmares. He was a killer. One who'd nearly destroyed both Nolan and her. One who had ended Nolan's father's life. And it gave her a heart-stopping jolt to see Donny Ray's name written on this woman's hand.

Nolan had likely had some heart-stopping moments, too. Along with some confusing ones.

You aren't Bill Dalton's son. You were never his son.

That's what Caroline had just told him. A message supposedly from the Grave Digger. But what did it mean? Better yet, why had the killer wanted Caroline to give that message to Nolan? Ditto for why the killer had included a photo of Nolan's father when he'd sent her a text.

"It's not true," Nolan said under his breath. He was obviously talking to himself, trying to piece this together just as Adalyn was doing. "I'm not adopted. He was my father."

Adalyn had no reason to doubt that. She'd heard Nolan talk about his dad, and they had been close. There had definitely been no mention of adoption. But maybe there was something to the revelation? Nolan's mother had been killed in a car accident when he was twelve so maybe she'd fathered him with another man and Bill had raised Nolan as his own.

"No," Nolan said as if reading her mind. "I've seen my birth certificate. Bill and Mary Dalton are my parents."

She didn't argue that birth certificates could be altered, but she could remind him of something else.

"The Grave Digger might be trying to mess with your head," Adalyn said. "He could want you to lose your focus so it'll be harder for you to catch him."

Though she couldn't figure out why the killer would have doled out something that could be disproven so easily. Nolan didn't have any siblings, but she recalled there were cousins on his father's side, and he could do a DNA comparison with one of them. For now though, they might be able to get more answers from Caroline.

"Do you know Donny Ray Carver?" Adalyn asked the woman.

Caroline groaned softly, turning her head from side to side. "Is he the one who took me? Was he the one who put me in this grave?"

"No," Adalyn answered. Because Donny Ray was in a maximum security prison awaiting an appeal for his conviction for murder. An appeal he wouldn't win.

But that didn't mean Donny Ray didn't have some kind of association with the Grave Digger. She just couldn't figure out a way to connect the dots right now.

Adalyn looked at Nolan to see if he had a better handle on this than she did, but one glimpse at his face, and she knew he didn't. Still, he might be able to do some dot connecting if she pushed a little.

"Has anything come up about Donny Ray in your investigation into the Grave Digger?" Adalyn whispered to him.

Before he could answer, she heard the sound of footsteps. Both Nolan and she reacted fast, drawing their guns and taking aim.

"It's me," Cody called out.

Nolan lowered his weapon, but Adalyn didn't until she saw that Cody was alone. Considering all the things that the Grave Digger had done, she wouldn't have put it past the snake to grab an FBI agent and use him as a human shield to continue whatever game he was playing. A game that might include killing them and the only woman who'd managed to survive being put in the ground.

Cody kept his eyes on Adalyn until she put away her gun in the slide holster at the back of her jeans, and he gave her a cool, disapproving look as he dropped the field kit bag on the ground next to Nolan.

"You got a permit for that gun?" Cody asked her.

Adalyn resisted huffing. *Really?* They were literally hovering over a woman who'd nearly been murdered and he was going to try to bust her chops over that?

"I have a permit," she assured him, using the same cool tone he had.

But there was heat inside her. Not the sexual kind of heat that had been between Nolan and her, either. No. This was the kind that reminded her that even though she did indeed have the permit, she wasn't a cop. Of course, Cody could point out that she'd voluntarily resigned from the force—and she had—but nothing less than resignation had been an option. Now, she was still trying to figure out how to deal with the consequences of what had happened.

While Nolan opened the field kit, Cody took out his phone and looked at the screen. "I did the search on Caroline Edmonson," Cody said.

At the mention of her name, Caroline opened her eyes again and focused on the agent.

"She's sixty-four, divorced, no kids," Cody continued. "Three days ago she was reported missing from Dark River, a small town up in Lubbock County."

"Three days?" Adalyn and Nolan repeated in unison. Caroline muttered it, too, along with shaking her head.

Where had the killer kept her all this time? And why had he taken her from Lubbock? That was nearly four hundred miles away, and all the other victims had come from the San Antonio area.

"He kidnapped me from my bedroom," the woman admitted. Tears spilled down both of her cheeks. Not calm, silent tears, either. Her breath started to hitch again. "I don't know when. There are so many blanks."

Probably because the killer had kept her drugged. Well, he had except for the time he'd had her memorizing what she was supposed to tell Nolan. A mind-clouding message no doubt meant to shock. Ditto for the notes penned on Caroline's palms.

Nolan, the lie you're living will kill you.

"Just stay calm," Nolan told Caroline when she tried to get up.

Since that didn't help, Adalyn touched the woman's fingers again. "It'll be okay," she tried to assure her. "All three of us are armed, and we aren't going to let anyone take you."

Squeezing her eyes against the tears, Caroline nodded. "I thought he was going to kill me."

Adalyn wouldn't mention that the Grave Digger had already done just that to other women, but while Nolan worked to remove the duct tape from her legs, Adalyn kept her focus on Caroline.

"Are you from Dark River?" Adalyn asked. The question earned her another cool look from Cody. Probably because he thought he should be the one asking questions. Maybe he was right, but it was obvious the woman was more comfortable with her than she was with the agents.

"I've lived there my whole life," Caroline murmured. Then, her eyes widened. "You said I'd been gone three days? Oh, God. Somebody needs to call Jeb and let him know I'm alive."

"Jeb?" Adalyn asked.

"Jeb Mercer," Caroline quickly supplied. "I'm his

cook and housekeeper. Have been for nearly forty years. He'll be so worried about me."

"Jeb Mercer?" Cody repeated, obviously recognizing the name. So did Adalyn. Even though Adalyn had never met him, he was somewhat of a Texas legend in law enforcement circles. "As in *Sheriff* Jeb Mercer?"

Caroline nodded. "He's retired now."

Adalyn hadn't known about the retirement, but then she didn't exactly move in those circles these days. Whoever had taken over for him certainly had big boots to fill.

"Please," Caroline pleaded. "Call Jeb and tell him I'm alive."

Cody and Nolan seemed to have a silent conversation with each other about that, and after Nolan gave the nod, Cody stepped away from them, no doubt to get in touch with Jeb Mercer.

"Mercer might have a connection to the Grave Digger," Nolan muttered, still tugging away at the duct tape. "Or to Donny Ray."

True. The retired sheriff had made some high-profile arrests, and many people called him the Law in Lubbock County. That caused a sickening feeling to settle over Adalyn. Maybe that's why Caroline had been taken? Because she worked for a cop with Mercer's reputation?

"I got Mercer's number," Cody relayed, dropping back down beside Nolan. He put on gloves from the field kit and helped with the tape. "Just tried it, but it went straight to voice mail."

"He'll be so worried," Caroline repeated. "And my kidnapping will stir up some bad memories for him."

That caused Nolan to stop and look at the woman. Cody, too. "How so?" Cody asked.

"A long time ago somebody kidnapped his little boy. Took him right from the ranch." Both her voice and her bottom lip trembled. "It broke Jeb's heart that they never found the boy."

Cody visibly relaxed, probably because he realized Caroline's comment about stirring up bad memories hadn't had anything to do with the Grave Digger. Not Nolan though. No relaxing for him. He turned back to removing the duct tape, but Adalyn could see the tense muscles in his jaw.

"If Mercer doesn't return my call before the ambulance gets here, I'll try him again," Cody assured Caroline. "Along with being your boss, is Mercer also your…partner or something?"

Cody no doubt wanted to know so he'd be prepared for how the retired sheriff would handle all of this.

Caroline shook her head as if she hadn't quite understood the question, and then it seemed to dawn on her. "No. Jeb's a dear friend. There's never been anything more than that between us."

Cody nodded and shifted his attention to Adalyn. "You might have already told Nolan this, but I'd like to hear it. What's your connection to the Grave Digger?" That sounded very much like an accusation. "It seems odd that he'd text you."

Odd didn't begin to describe it. But Adalyn had

given it some thought on the frantic drive from San Antonio to the Hill Country trail where the Grave Digger had instructed her to go.

"I don't have a connection that I know of. I'll go back through my old case files," she said. "I didn't deal with a killer with his MO, but maybe there was something." Heck, she could have investigated him before he came up with his "signature" of leaving his victims in graves. "I doubt he just plucked my name out of a hat."

"No," Nolan agreed. "But you have a connection to me, and it's obvious he wants me at the center of this. *Whatever this is*," he added in a growl.

Yes, that was true. Nolan and she hadn't kept their past relationship a secret, and it had come out when the media was covering his father's murder. Maybe the Grave Digger intended for her to be another diversion for him. Another way to mess with his head. If so, it seemed to be working. She knew Nolan enough to see that he was indeed distracted.

"Are you close to IDing the Grave Digger?" Adalyn came out and asked. "Because what he's doing seems almost desperate." Which, of course, could be some kind of calculation.

Nolan lifted his shoulder, but before he could say anything, there was the howl of a siren. The ambulance. Maybe even backup and the ERT. Adalyn welcomed both because it would get Caroline the medical help she needed, and the ERT might be able to find something to give them answers.

"Go ahead and bag Caroline's hands," Nolan instructed Cody. "I want her fingernails checked for any trace."

"He washed my hands," Caroline blurted out. "He put me in a bathtub and scrubbed me from head to toe."

Obviously, Caroline was remembering things. It might only be bits and pieces, but more might come when her mind cleared. More that could lead the FBI to the Grave Digger. Something that Adalyn very much wanted to happen. She had a personal stake in this investigation now. The killer had seen to that by sending her here and putting her in the middle of it.

Cody stood after he finished bagging Caroline's hand. "I'll go back to the road and lead the EMTs here," Cody volunteered. "You'll be okay?" he added to Nolan.

Adalyn didn't think she'd mistaken Cody's tone. Not a friendly one. And he was basically asking Nolan if it was all right to leave him with a woman who could have had something to do with Caroline being in that grave. Obviously, Adalyn hadn't convinced him of her innocence when he'd asked her about that text.

"I'll be fine," Nolan said, almost absently.

Yeah, the Grave Digger had definitely caused a distraction. One that could turn out to be deadly because he could be using this as a ploy to kill again.

Cody stared at Nolan a few seconds, shrugged and then headed back toward the clearing. Toward the sound of the sirens that were getting closer. He'd been gone only a few seconds when there was another sound.

Footsteps.

Not from the direction Cody had gone. These were coming from the trail that Adalyn had taken.

Nolan tossed aside the evidence bag he'd been using to collect the duct tape, and he stood and drew his gun. Shoulder to shoulder with him, Adalyn did the same. They both took aim at the lanky man who pushed away a tree branch and made a beeline toward them.

"Is she alive?" the man immediately demanded. "Is Caroline all right?"

"Jeb," Caroline called out, and she started struggling to get to a sitting position.

Since Adalyn didn't want the woman aggravating any possible injuries, she stooped down to keep Caroline in place. But Adalyn also kept her eye on the man. He was in his sixties, probably close to the same age as Caroline, and the hair that peeked out from beneath his Stetson was iron gray. Despite his age and rail-thin body, he still looked formidable. Ditto for the Smith & Wesson that he wore like an Old West gunslinger in a hip holster.

"You're Jeb Mercer?" Adalyn asked.

"Yeah." He barely spared Adalyn a glance. Instead, he dropped down on his knees beside Caroline and reached out as if to pull her into his arms. His cop's training must have kicked in though because he stopped. "You're alive." The muscles stirred in his wrinkled face. "Did that bastard hurt you?"

Caroline managed to shake her head. "I'm all right. Now that you're here, I'm all right."

Jeb groaned, obviously not at all certain that his housekeeper was indeed okay. Still, he stood to face Nolan and her. "I'm going with Caroline to the hospital." He said it like a challenge, but there was no challenge in his expression when it landed on Nolan. Jeb's breath seemed to rattle in his chest, and his weathered brown eyes widened.

"I thought it was a lie," Jeb murmured, staggering back a step. "I thought it was all a lie."

Nolan cursed. "What the hell are you talking about? And what are you doing here? How did you know where to find Caroline?" His tone was more like Cody's now. An FBI agent interrogating a suspect.

It took Jeb a moment to answer, and Adalyn could see that the man was struggling to keep his composure. His reaction hadn't been this extreme when he'd first seen Caroline, but he'd sure reached the extreme level now that he was looking at Nolan.

"I got two texts from a man who says he took Caroline," Jeb said without taking his eyes off Nolan. "He claimed he was a serial killer and gave me a map where I could find her."

He paused, and it seemed to Adalyn that he was trying to blink back tears. His hands were trembling. Definitely not the demeanor of the formidable cop who'd arrived just moments earlier.

"He also said I'd find my son here," Jeb added, and there was more breath than sound in his voice. It was trembling, too.

"Your son?" Nolan challenged.

Jeb nodded. "My son. *You*."

Chapter Three

Nolan fought against the punch of shock and dread he felt. Fought because this was no place for such things.

For such lies.

Because everything Jeb Mercer had just said was all a distraction, one no doubt designed by the Grave Digger to stir up enough confusion so that Nolan would let down his guard.

It was easier to kill a lawman when his guard was down.

And it was obvious that Mercer was just as much of a victim as Caroline had been. The Grave Digger had likely wanted Mercer to suffer. But why? Maybe when Nolan figured out that connection, it could end up being a deadly blow to the serial killer. This many pieces could maybe lead them to figuring out his identity.

"I'm not your son," Nolan told Mercer. "I'm Special Agent Nolan Dalton."

He'd managed to keep some of the emotion out of his voice, barely, and he'd managed it while making some sweeping glances around them. This would be the perfect time for the Grave Digger to attack.

Mercer certainly wasn't doing any glancing around. He kept his attention fixed to Nolan. "Yes, you are my son." He groaned and pressed his fists against the sides of his head.

"Is he Joe?" Caroline asked. She, too, was staring at Nolan, and as she was reaching for Jeb, she tried to get up again. Thankfully, Adalyn kept the woman in place. "Is he Joe?" she repeated.

Apparently, that was the name of Mercer's son who'd been kidnapped. The only thing Nolan knew about that particular kidnapping was what he'd learned minutes earlier from Caroline and Jeb Mercer. Which wasn't much. But it didn't matter because he wasn't Joe Mercer. He was Bill Dalton's son.

"Your eyes," Jeb muttered, but that's all he said for several crawling seconds. "They're identical to mine and my other two kids. You have a brother and sister, and you were taken from me. From them."

The man's voice cracked, and he finally looked away but not before Nolan saw tears shimmering in those very eyes that Jeb had just claimed were a genetic match. So what if his eyes were brown? It was a common color, and it proved nothing.

"The Grave Digger likes to play games," Nolan assured him. "This is just one more of them."

Jeb opened his mouth, probably to dispute that, but Cody's voice stopped him. "It's me," Cody announced, probably so they wouldn't draw weapons on him. "I've got the EMTs with me."

Before Cody had even finished speaking, he came through the trees and underbrush, and there were indeed two EMTs right behind him. The EMTs went straight to Caroline, but Cody hung back a little, and he volleyed looks at Jeb, Nolan and Adalyn before his attention finally settled on Jeb.

"Sheriff Mercer?" Cody asked. When Jeb only nodded, Cody turned to Nolan. "What's going on? Why is he here?"

"More mind games," Nolan snarled like profanity. "The Grave Digger sent Sheriff Mercer two texts." That was all the time and explanation Nolan was going to give this. When he turned to Jeb, he shoved everything aside and did his job.

"We'll need to take your phone," Nolan told Jeb. "We'll want to analyze the texts. What did the killer tell you about Caroline?" Best to limit the interview to just the woman and the texts. For now anyway.

"That he had her, and if I wanted to find her, I'd come to San Antonio right away," Jeb answered. "He said if I told anyone or brought anyone with me that he'd kill her."

So, the last part was similar to what the Grave Digger had threatened in the text he'd sent Nolan.

"I left within minutes," Jeb continued. "And no, I didn't call anyone, but I did leave a message at my house just in case something went wrong and I didn't… Well, in case something went wrong," he settled for saying. "My other son and daughter are both cops. Trust me, it was hard to hold off telling them, but I didn't know if this so-called Grave Digger had a way of monitoring communications."

Nolan didn't like the possibility of that, but maybe

the Grave Digger had managed to get cameras or listening devices in both Jeb's and his houses. Then again, the threat could have been just part of the game as well. Maybe it didn't matter to the Grave Digger if they'd gotten to Caroline in time or not.

"I didn't get the second text from him until I was in San Antonio," Jeb went on. He paused again and took a couple of sharp breaths. "That's the one that told me about you. And how to get here."

Again, Nolan just pushed aside the *told me about you* and continued the interview. "Were there any photos attached to either of the texts?" He'd check for himself, along with having the messages analyzed, but he needed to hear Jeb's take on what he'd received.

Jeb nodded again, took out his phone and handed it to Nolan, who immediately put it in an evidence bag.

"There's a picture of Caroline with the second text." Jeb cursed under his breath. "She's wearing a blindfold and a gag, but I knew it was her. There's also one of…my son Joe. It was taken right before he was kidnapped a little over twenty-seven years ago. He was three and a half at the time." The man paused a heartbeat. "How old are you, Special Agent Dalton?"

Nolan had just turned thirty-one, which meant the math worked. Of course, it did. The Grave Digger would have made sure of that. No need to set up a ruse that could be easily dispelled. But Nolan had no intention of confirming his age or anything else to Jeb.

"Did you come here from Lubbock County?" Nolan asked Jeb. When the man nodded, Nolan went with a follow-up even though he already knew the answer because of the time stamp on the message. "When did you get the first text?"

"Early this morning. About six and a half hours ago. The text said Caroline would die if I didn't get here so I left the message at my house, got in my truck and started driving. When I was about fifty miles out, I got the second text." He stopped again. "I had to pull over to read it, and it took me a couple of minutes before I could start driving again."

A couple of minutes that the lawman had no doubt needed to compose himself. Nolan silently cursed the Grave Digger for putting Jeb through that. The memories of losing his son had to be a nightmare for him, and the text would have brought it all back to the surface.

Nolan shifted his attention to Adalyn. "I'll need your phone, too," Nolan told her because she, too, had a text and photos that would need to be processed by the crime lab.

She handed her phone to Nolan, while watching Jeb and him. Adalyn was no doubt trying to see if those eyes were indeed a match or if there was a family resemblance.

Cody cleared his throat, breaking the uncomfortable silence. "I spotted a camera right over there."

That got Nolan's attention, and he followed the direction of Cody's pointing finger to a large oak that was only about ten feet away. Nolan did indeed see a small black lens attached to one of the thick branches.

"I think the SOB was watching us the whole time," Cody snarled. "Hell, he's probably still watching us.

There are some wires attached to the camera, and I didn't know if it was rigged to some kind of device that would destroy it if I touched it. I'll let the ERT handle it when they get here."

A good decision on Cody's part. Not on the killer's though to leave something like that for them to find. Because it was yet another piece they could use in this puzzle to learn more about him.

The Grave Digger had never given them this much of himself before. Texts, pictures, the camera—and a live witness. Nolan wanted to spend some time thinking about why the killer had done that. Was it just more of the game? Or had he gotten cocky and taken risks that could land his sorry butt in jail?

Nolan was hoping it was the latter.

But even if it wasn't, at least he was mentally on the right track now. He was thinking about how to approach this leg of the investigation, and that was a far better thing for him to dwell on rather than the lies the Grave Digger had doled out to Sheriff Mercer.

Nolan didn't blame Jeb for believing those lies since it was obvious the man was desperate to find his kidnapped son, and the killer had played on that desperation. In doing so, he'd also muddied the already murky waters because there was a ton of new evidence that would need to be studied and processed. Jeb Mercer was now part of that evidence, but Nolan would keep some distance from him. No need to keep tormenting the man with the lie—especially since they didn't know the reason the Grave Digger had dropped the fake bombshell.

Cody took over bagging the phones while Nolan gave instructions to the EMTs. "This woman's name is Caroline Edmondson," Nolan told them. "She's the survivor of an abduction by a serial killer, and everything she's wearing needs to be examined for evidence and trace. She's not to be left alone at any time. Understand?"

The EMTs gave him nods of assurance, but Nolan took that one step further. He got the name of the San Antonio hospital where she'd be transported, and he arranged for two FBI agents to meet the ambulance. Nolan didn't want the Grave Digger to get a chance to finish what he'd started.

"Backup is still at least fifteen minutes out," Cody said, checking his watch. "If you're okay staying here at the scene with Adalyn and Sheriff Mercer, I can go with Caroline in the ambulance."

Nolan wasn't at all comfortable about being with Jeb, but the man spoke before Nolan could say anything. "I need to follow the ambulance to the hospital," Jeb insisted. "I heard you say it was North Central Baptist," he added to Nolan. "I'll hurry back to my truck and put that in my GPS. I want Caroline to be with someone she knows."

"No, Jeb," Caroline argued as the EMTs put her on a stretcher. "Stay here with him," she insisted, motioning to Nolan. Obviously, she was saying that because she believed Nolan was Jeb's long-lost son. "You can come to the hospital later."

Since Nolan could practically feel the debate Jeb was having with himself as to what he should do, he solved the dilemma for the man. "Go with Caroline," Nolan instructed. "Either Special Agent Hill or one of the other FBI agents will take your statement."

Jeb still didn't jump on that order to leave. He waited, his attention fixed on Nolan, and it was obvious what he wanted. Some kind of acknowledgment that there was at least a kernel of truth in what the Grave Digger had told him. It was an acknowledgment that Nolan couldn't give him.

"My DNA is on file," Jeb finally said to Nolan. "Yours will be, too. Compare them. *Please.*" The moment he'd gotten out that last word, he hurried away, no doubt heading to his truck.

Nolan considered giving Jeb a warning to be careful, but the Grave Digger had already had ample opportunity to kill the lawman. Plus, if he hadn't wanted Jeb as part of this scenario he'd set in motion, the killer wouldn't have sent him those two texts.

"Are you okay?" Adalyn asked him. Except she didn't just ask the question. She reached out, touched his arm and rubbed softly. A gesture meant to soothe and comfort. And it did.

Some.

But it did something else. It reminded Nolan of the times when they'd done a whole lot more than just touch.

He cursed again, but this time he didn't keep the words to himself. Nolan spit them out, frustrated that he'd even think of that now. Of course, the Grave Digger was probably loving the fact that he was messing with Nolan's head.

"I'm all right," Nolan told her.

She made a sound implying she didn't quite buy that. And she kept touching. Slow, soft strokes. "Is it possible you're Jeb's son?"

"No. It's a lie," Nolan insisted. Hell. It had to be. But he'd look into it, along with all the other things the Grave Digger had said. "I'm not comparing my DNA though. No need to tie up lab resources for something like that."

Adalyn kept her eyes on him but finally drew back her hand. "Comparing the DNA might give you some peace of mind by confirming it's a lie."

"I already have peace of mind," he snarled. Of course, that dripped with sarcasm because there wasn't much peace anywhere in his life. He was tracking down a vicious killer who didn't mind slinging Nolan's personal life around.

Or Adalyn's.

Because, after all, she'd been dragged into this as well.

"I know you said you didn't know why you got the text about Caroline, but before today, did you have any reason to believe you were on the Grave Digger's radar?" he asked.

"No," she answered quickly, but then she hesitated. Adalyn shook her head. "Maybe it's just a hindsight-being-twenty-twenty deal, but looking back, I had the feeling I was being watched. Nothing more than a feeling," she added. "How about you? Has the Grave Digger sent you other texts?"

"He has, but the others were to inform me of the

locations of the bodies. And this was the first time he's included pictures and other people."

"Yes," she murmured. "Other people who'll have to give statements. What Jeb said about believing you're his son will become part of the official record. Ditto for our past relationship. So, maybe he's trying to get you discredited in some way. Maybe get you removed from the investigation. That's why I asked you if you were close to IDing him."

Nolan hadn't believed he was close to doing that, but now he needed to take another look. At everything.

His phone dinged with a text. Normally, it wasn't a sound that caused his body to brace, but it did now. And Nolan braced even more when he saw the message from the unknown number.

It's not a lie, the text said. But why don't I spill some of your blood so you'll have something to compare to good ole Sheriff Mercer?

Hell. Nolan automatically took hold of Adalyn's arm to move her to cover, but it was already too late.

The blast slammed into them.

Chapter Four

Adalyn felt as if a speeding Mack truck had just rammed into her back. She flew forward and then her chest, arms, knees and forehead hit the ground. Hard. The jolt knocked the breath right out of her. But it didn't knock away the pain. No. She immediately felt plenty of that at every point of impact.

She heard herself groan, a sound that was barely audible because she was still fighting for air, and she rolled onto her side so she could try to get to her feet. Despite the pain, she was thinking clearly enough to know one thing.

Someone had just tried to kill them.

And that someone could already be moving in closer to finish them off.

Beside her, Nolan groaned as well. And he cursed all the while struggling to stand up. The moment he managed to do that, he took hold of her arm, and they started running. Well, running as much as they could manage. Gasping and panting, they limped to get behind the cover of a large tree.

"The camera," Nolan spit out. "It blew up."

Because her head was still spinning, it took Adalyn a moment to process what he'd said, but yes, it had indeed exploded. There was nothing left of it or the tree branch where the camera had been mounted. There wasn't much left of the tree, either, and the debris was now scattered all over the crime scene. If the Grave Digger had left any useful evidence behind, they weren't likely to find it now. It'd be like looking for a needle in a haystack.

And speaking of haystacks, that's how Adalyn saw the dozens and dozens of trees and shrubs around them. The killer could be there, hiding behind any one of them, so she forced herself to pick through their surroundings and look. Focus. But she didn't see anyone. Didn't hear anyone, either, but her ears were still ringing and her heartbeat thudding so it was hard to hear much of anything.

Adalyn finally managed to drag in a much-needed breath, taking in the stench that was now heavy in the air. Everything smelled scorched, and she soon spotted the source of that. There were some sparks with small coils of smoke scattered around them. However, since the ground was still damp from a recent rain, the sparks quickly died out and didn't grow into full-fledged flames.

Thank goodness.

That was something at least. She certainly didn't want to be caught in the middle of a fire. Plus, a fire would make it next to impossible for the ERT to examine whatever pieces of the camera they could find.

Those pieces could lead to the identity of the person who'd put it there.

Could.

But again, Adalyn knew they couldn't count on that. Right now, the killer was in control and calling the shots. That had to stop.

"Are you hurt?" Nolan asked her.

Parts of her were still throbbing from the fall, but Adalyn didn't think she had any serious injuries so she shook her head. "You?"

Muttering some profanity, he rotated his shoulder, testing it. And wincing with the test. "I'm all right," he said, not sounding very convincing.

Nolan's face had some nicks and bruises, but she didn't see any deep wounds. Still, that didn't mean he didn't have some internal injuries. Ditto for her. But right now dealing with their injuries wasn't on the top of her list of things they had to do to survive this.

"We shouldn't stay here," she muttered, still keeping watch around them.

He made a quick sound of agreement. "There could be another explosive."

That sent her heart into overdrive. Obviously, the killer had had some time in these woods while he'd been burying Caroline and setting up that camera with the explosive. He'd probably spent hours here. So, yes, he could have set up other bombs as well.

"Keep watch behind us," Nolan instructed, and he got them moving.

Adalyn soon realized that her right knee was throbbing, probably from a deep bruise. The bone wasn't broken—she was sure of that—so she tried not to think of the pain while she plowed past the fallen limbs and jagged pieces of wood with Nolan leading the way.

He followed the path that Cody and he had made when they'd rushed to the scene. No doubt because there were no visible explosives or other cameras on the path. Of course, the killer could have hidden something. Something that could and would blow them to smithereens.

But she didn't think so.

"He could have killed us at any time," Adalyn muttered. She was talking to herself, trying to put the pieces of the puzzle together, but she soon realized that Nolan had heard her.

"Yeah," he agreed. "At any time."

While that wasn't exactly a comforting thought, it gave her a piece of the puzzle. Well, maybe it did. If the Grave Digger didn't want them dead, not yet anyway, then he wanted to keep them alive for something. Maybe just to keep playing this sick game with them? But it could be more than that.

More connected to Jeb Mercer and the child who'd been stolen from him nearly thirty years ago.

The child who could be Nolan.

No way would Adalyn bring that up now. Too much of a distraction, but she had no doubts that it was heavy on his mind. Once he got past the emotion of dealing with it, Nolan would see that the Grave Digger had a motive for dropping that bombshell. To taunt Nolan and muddy the waters of the investigation. Perhaps to taunt Jeb, too, and that brought her back to the possibility that Nolan was close to IDing the killer.

She continued to keep watch behind them while they ran, but Adalyn saw no one. Still, she stayed vigilant with her gun ready when they reached the black SUV parked on the narrow dirt road. Nolan used the keypad to unlock the doors, and they both practically dived inside.

"Are these windows bullet resistant?" she immediately asked.

Still breathing hard, Nolan nodded, started the engine and drove off. Not far though. He went to a spot about fifty yards away to a clear enough area where he could turn around. Adalyn kept watch there, too, because she wouldn't put it past the killer to try to ambush them when they thought they were on the verge of getting to safety.

But there'd be no safe place.

Not really. Not as long as the Grave Digger was out there.

"I'm heading to the hospital," he muttered, and like her, he was volleying glances all around them. "I need to question Caroline."

Yes, he did. It was one of those boxes that had to be ticked off even though Adalyn figured the woman had already told them all she could. And the bits and pieces she'd told them were actually a lot.

"If the killer wore a mask," Adalyn said, speculating now, "he probably intended all along for her to stay alive."

"Alive while he had her and while she was in the

ground," Nolan answered. "Now that she's delivered his so-called message, he might want to kill her so as not to spoil his *perfect* record."

That caused some fresh fear to slide through her, and the possibility of something like that happening was probably also the reason Nolan used his hands-free to make a call to Cody. Or rather try to make a call. Adalyn heard when it went straight to voice mail, but Nolan left a message to tell Cody what'd happened with the camera. He also reminded Cody to make sure Caroline stayed protected at all times.

"Have someone keep an eye on Jeb Mercer, too," Nolan added to Cody right before he ended the voice mail.

Because the killer might not be finished with Jeb's part in this as well. But exactly what part Jeb had played, Adalyn still didn't know.

"The timing of the texts that Jeb got indicate the killer contacted him before he'd even put Caroline in the grave," she said mentally going through the timeline.

It was something that Nolan had no doubt already realized, but she was hoping by just repeating it aloud that it would spur something to help them figure out what the heck was going on.

"The killer wanted to give Jeb time to get here and arrive on scene," Nolan added. He gave her a quick glance, only a split second, but it was long enough for her to see the questions and the concern brewing in his eyes. "On scene with me," he emphasized. "And maybe with you. I need to check your phone, but it appears the killer texted you and me around the same time."

True. Which meant the Grave Digger had also wanted her on scene with Nolan, Cody, Caroline and Jeb.

"I don't know why he'd do that," she volunteered. "The only thing I can come up with is that I'm a distraction. *Your* distraction. And that's also why the killer wrote Donny Ray's name on Caroline's hand. The Grave Digger wants you focusing on your father's murder and not on him."

Nolan didn't argue with any of that, but the muscles in his forehead were bunched up as if he was giving her words plenty of thought. She certainly was. Because Donny Ray wasn't just a part of something that'd happened in Nolan's life. The man was also a big part of hers.

Still was.

He was the reason she was no longer a cop. The reason she still couldn't sleep without the nightmares taking over.

"I didn't know anything about the abduction of Jeb's son," Adalyn went on. "And before today, I'd never laid eyes on Caroline or Jeb. So, why else would the Grave Digger want me in these woods with you? Unless..." She paused. "Maybe I was supposed to die when the camera exploded. That would have messed with your head some."

This time, his glance was slightly longer. "Some," he repeated with plenty of heat in his voice. Not attraction heat but rather anger. Maybe because she'd minimized the effect her death would have on him. Or maybe because Nolan didn't like her being used as a pawn to get to him. Well, Adalyn sure as heck didn't like it, either.

Nolan finally reached the end of the dirt trail and turned onto a road that would take them to the interstate. There weren't nearly as many trees or places for a killer to hide on this particular route, but Adalyn kept watch anyway. She also looked for other vehicles because the Grave Digger could still be lurking around. He'd used some kind of transportation to get Caroline all the way out here, and he might have stayed back, waiting for Nolan, or her, to leave so he could move on to the next step of whatever chaos he was trying to stir up.

"You'll need to take precautions," Nolan said, pulling her attention back to him. "You're similar, physically, to the Grave Digger's victims. More than Caroline. And we don't know specifically how he takes the women. It's possible he's using hired muscle for that. Muscle that he could already have in place when it comes to you being a target."

Well, that was a stark reminder that would stay in her head. Which was no doubt why Nolan had said it. He didn't want her getting careless, the way she'd done when his father had been killed. The possibility of Donny Ray attacking her hadn't even been on her radar. If it had been, if she'd been looking out for him, Nolan's father might still be alive.

"If you want, you can stay at my house for a while," Nolan continued. "Until we can get a handle on this."

He didn't sound especially pleased about having made that offer. Adalyn wasn't especially pleased about taking him up on it, either. But it was something she'd consider. She valued her privacy—and keeping some space between Nolan and her to stave off this attraction. However, it'd be stupid to put either of those things above her safety. Because if she was in danger, so was Nolan. She was certain of that.

"I'll think about it," she let him know and then added, "Thank you."

He muttered something she didn't catch just as the ringing sound shot through the SUV. Adalyn hadn't needed anything to remind her that she was right on the edge, but that did it. She gasped before she could get her survival instincts to register that the sound wasn't a threat. It was just Nolan's phone ringing.

"It's Cody," he relayed to her, and he put the call on speaker.

"Got your voice mail," Cody said, adding a few curse words. "The camera really blew up?"

"It did," Nolan verified. "The crime scene's a mess."

"And what about Adalyn and you? Are you both all right?"

"All right enough." Nolan glanced at her again. "But Adalyn should be checked out when we get to the hospital."

"I can arrange that," Cody volunteered. "For you, too."

"Focus on Adalyn and keeping Caroline safe," Nolan insisted.

"Will do. We just got to the hospital, and I'm keeping my eyes on her while she's being taken into an exam room." Cody paused. "A piece of paper fell out of her bra when the EMTs were moving her. It's basically a typed recap of the message Caroline gave us at the scene. I'm guessing the killer did that in case she died and didn't get a chance to personally relay the message to you."

That was Adalyn's guess as well. They'd had to do CPR to get Caroline breathing, but if they'd failed to save her, the Grave Digger would have wanted a backup way to torment and confuse them.

"Anything in the recap message about Donny Ray Carver?" Nolan asked Cody.

"No." Cody sighed. "But after Caroline's been examined, I'll see if I can press her on that. I'm sorry, Nolan," he added. "I know this is stirring up a lot of bad stuff for you. Gotta go," Cody said before Nolan could respond. "Sheriff Mercer just came running in, and the security guard stopped him. I'll clear his path so he can see Caroline. I think it'll steady her to have him here."

Cody ended the call, and both Nolan and she sat in silence, obviously going over everything they'd just heard. It would indeed steady Caroline to have Jeb with her, but it definitely wouldn't do anything of the kind for Nolan. Adalyn could see the way all of this was working on him. Scattering his focus. Which was almost certainly the intent of the killer.

But what if it was more than that?

Adalyn tried to approach that question from several angles and came up with nothing. Well, nothing logical anyway.

"Maybe the Grave Digger had something to do with taking Jeb's son?" she threw out there. "Or he could have come in contact with the person who did it. If so, that means he could have connections to Lubbock."

Nolan made a sound that could have meant anything. He certainly didn't jump to agree with her, and even if he had, it likely wouldn't have taken them anywhere. Still, she intended to get access to databases at Secure Point, where she worked. She could do some general searches for similar crimes and such.

"I'll search the files and see if any of the persons of interest are from Lubbock or spent any time there," he muttered seconds later as he took the turn onto the interstate. He hit the sirens and sped up.

"Persons of interest?" she repeated. "Who?"

He scowled, probably because he obviously hadn't intended to share that with her. "Just people who are linked in some way to the other five victims. Ex-boyfriends, wannabe boyfriends, disgruntled coworkers, that sort of thing."

Since she'd been a cop, Adalyn knew all of that had to be checked out even if for no other reason than to eliminate them. "Are there any persons of interest who overlap all five women?"

The glance he gave her was flat. All FBI. And she was certain that meant he would clam up. But he didn't.

"No," Nolan finally said. "Nothing overlaps except

for them being killed by the same person. Or some-one using the same MO anyway."

Adalyn jumped right on that. "You think it's pos-sible you have a copycat? Or two killers?"

"No," he repeated. "I believe it's one killer. One sick, very twisted SOB, and with the exception of Car-oline, he likes to murder women...who look like you."

Even though he'd already mentioned that, spelling it out still hit home. Another of those gut punches, and she'd already had too many of them for one day.

"Everything about you fits," Nolan went on. "You're young, just turned thirty. Brown hair, blue eyes. The other victims either had and were still in jobs where they were in authority. For instance, a CEO of a family business, a school principal, a for-mer military cop."

Yeah, definitely another punch. "So, why not try to take me instead of Caroline? He could have had me deliver the message to you. Could have still come up with something that would have gotten Jeb to come all the way down from Lubbock."

Nolan didn't speculate on the answer, and she was partly thankful for that. With her stomach already doing flip-flops, it was probably best for him not to spell out that the Grave Digger wasn't finished.

That she could still be the serial killer's next target.

At the speed Nolan was going, it didn't take them that long to reach the exit to the hospital, and he kept the sirens blaring as he pulled into the parking lot.

But his weren't the only sirens. Other vehicles were racing toward the hospital.

Cops.

Plenty of them.

Nolan pulled to a quick stop and called Cody, who answered on the first ring. "We've got a problem," Cody immediately said. "An orderly found what appears to be a bomb in the ER. I've got to get Caroline out of here right now."

Chapter Five

Nolan's instinct was to run into the hospital and help Cody get Caroline out of there, but he made himself stay put in the parking lot for a couple of seconds.

And he thought this through.

The bomb could be a way for the Grave Digger to finish off Caroline, but it could also be a way of getting to Adalyn and him. Maybe this was just another round of taunting, but it could also be the real deal. The Grave Digger might be ready to try to put an end to their lives.

"Keep watch," Nolan instructed Adalyn, but it was something she was already doing.

"You said the SUV was bullet resistant," she muttered with her gaze firing all around them. "Maybe Cody should put Caroline in here? At least until we're sure this isn't a hoax."

Nolan made a quick sound of agreement. Though he figured the medical staff wouldn't think it was a good plan. The hospital had measures in place for the evacuation, but that no doubt involved hurrying to get everyone out as fast and orderly as possible.

That gave the Grave Digger way too much access to the only one of his victims to ever survive.

"Stay put," Nolan instructed Adalyn when he spotted Cody coming out of the ER. Cody had his left arm looped around Caroline's waist. Jeb was doing the same thing on the other side of her.

Jeb.

Of course.

He should have known the man would be with her, and that meant Jeb would likely also be getting into the SUV. Nolan would have preferred to keep his distance so there'd be no chance of him bringing up that whole lost-son/resemblance thing, but this wasn't the time for distancing. Because Jeb might also be a target. He might need the bullet resistant vehicle just as much as Caroline.

There was a nurse behind Caroline, and while Nolan couldn't hear every word she said, she was demanding that Cody take Caroline toward the side entrance. Probably where the staff was setting up a triage area. An area that would keep Caroline out in the open for what could turn out to be deadly minutes, since Cody would have to walk over there with her in tow.

Nolan called out to Cody and motioned for them to head their way. They did. Cody flashed his badge to the nurse, but then he immediately put it away so he could keep his right hand over his gun. Nolan bolted out of the SUV and opened the back door so they could all hurry to get in.

Caroline didn't look any steadier than she had at

the crime scene. Neither did Jeb, and the man's attention went straight to Nolan the moment he was back behind the wheel.

"What happened to you two?" Jeb asked, his gaze volleying between Adalyn and Nolan. "How were you hurt?"

Nolan frowned and actually debated whether he should even answer that. But it seemed petty to hold back this kind of info when it was obvious that Jeb was concerned.

"There was an explosive device in the woods," Nolan settled for explaining, and he tried to choose his words carefully. He figured it wouldn't help Caroline to have her refer to it as the *grave site*.

Even with Nolan toning it down though, the color still drained from Caroline's face. "Maybe the killer thought I was still there." Her words rushed out with her breath. "Maybe he was trying to make sure I was dead."

Nolan shook his head, started the engine and drove to the back corner of the parking lot. Still close enough to the hospital if Caroline ended up needing immediate attention from the medical personnel but also far enough from the building in case there truly was an explosion.

As he'd pointed out to Adalyn, the SUV was reinforced so they wouldn't be gunned down while inside it, but they might need to get Caroline to another hospital. Nolan checked the GPS to locate the nearest one in case it became necessary. For now though,

Cody and he could stay close enough until there was more law enforcement on the scene.

"The bomb was rigged to a camera," Cody explained, meeting Nolan's gaze in the mirror. "I don't think the Grave Digger was after you, or he would have set it off while you were still there."

Caroline squeezed her eyes shut a moment. "But he's not finished with me." She dropped her head onto Jeb's shoulder, and the man's arm went around her in a comforting gesture. "He had me pass along that message," Caroline added in a murmur, "but he's not finished."

Nolan wished he could dispute that, but he was very much afraid that Caroline was right. And once the Grave Digger had used her for whatever else he intended, then he might try to murder her. And that brought Nolan back to the killer's motives and why he'd used Caroline, Adalyn and Jeb in the first place.

Behind them, the chaos of the evacuation was in full swing with sirens screaming and people scrambling. Nolan didn't dismiss any of that, and he kept on the lookout for any signs they were about to be attacked, but he also turned in the seat and looked at Jeb.

"I'm not your son," Nolan started, and he hoped he sounded a lot more convinced of that than he felt. "But obviously the Grave Digger wants you to believe I am. Why?" And Nolan left his simple question at that.

Jeb shifted on the seat, and he groaned. "I don't know. Maybe the Grave Digger's connected to one of my old cases. Or to one of yours." He lifted Caroline's hand where the name was still written. "Donny Ray Carver. I called an old friend while I was driving to the hospital and asked for a quick background on the guy. He's appealing his sentence while he's on death row."

If Jeb had learned that, then he knew why Donny Ray had gotten that particular sentence. But before Nolan could say anything, Adalyn filled him in.

"Donny Ray was gunning for me, and he killed Nolan's father instead." She stopped and gathered her breath. "Have you ever crossed paths with him?"

Jeb stayed quiet a moment as if giving that some thought. "I don't think so, but my friend is sending me his photo. That might jog something."

Nolan decided to speed things up. He used his phone to pull up Donny Ray's picture and showed it to Jeb.

Jeb took the phone, studying the screen for several long moments. "He looks familiar," he mumbled. "But I can't place him. I'll need to go through my files and see if anything pops. How about you? Do you recognize him?" he asked Caroline.

Caroline looked at the screen, too. Just a glance. And she frantically shook her head. "No," she insisted before her gaze darted away.

Nolan continued to stare at the woman, hoping for more and wondering what the hell that reaction was all about. Maybe it was because Donny Ray's name was now associated with the Grave Digger. But maybe it was something else.

"You're sure you don't know him?" Nolan pressed.

"Positive," Caroline blurted out. "I just don't want to think about any of this right now. I want to stop hearing his voice."

Nolan doubted she was talking about Donny Ray but rather the Grave Digger. Still, he'd push her further once Caroline had gotten the all clear from her doctor. Obviously though, Cody intended to get some answers.

"Until you got that text from the Grave Digger, did you have any idea where your missing son was?" Cody asked Jeb.

The man lifted his shoulder, but there was nothing casual about the shrug, and Nolan didn't think it was his imagination that Jeb purposely didn't look at him. "We've had some leads over the years, but they've all fizzled out."

"Any of the leads connect to San Antonio, the FBI or the Grave Digger?" Cody added.

"None that immediately come to mind, but I'll do some checking there, too. A lot of the older files aren't in the computer, but I've got copies at my house. My daughter, Leigh, is the sheriff now, and she could maybe start going through them. I was going to call her anyway and tell her everything that's going on."

Everything would no doubt include the Grave Digger's claim that Nolan was the long-lost Joe Mercer. Nolan hoped that didn't mean he'd soon get a visit from this Leigh or Jeb's son.

Nolan's phone rang, but he didn't recognize the number. "This is Russell Mason," the caller immediately said. "I'm Adalyn's boss, and I need to speak to her now."

Frowning, Nolan passed the phone to her. "Your boss," he relayed and noticed that Adalyn's mouth tightened more than a little.

"Sorry," she said to Russell, "but this isn't a good time—"

"What the hell happened to you? Are you all right?" Russell demanded, and even though she hadn't put the call on speaker, Nolan had no trouble hearing the man.

Adalyn rubbed her hand over her face and winced, probably because she'd irritated one of the small cuts she'd sustained in the blast. "I'm fine. What have you heard?"

"That you're involved in the Grave Digger investigation," her boss immediately said.

Adalyn groaned. "And how did you hear that?"

"It's all over the news. Turn on any local channel, and you'll see it. Someone sent footage of you digging a woman out of a shallow grave in the woods."

Adalyn looked at Nolan, and he saw the shock and then the anger flare in her eyes. Nolan figured there was plenty of anger in his, too. The SOB killer had indeed been watching them and now had put a nightmare out there for people to view like entertainment.

"There was a message with the footage that you were assisting the FBI," Russell continued. "That you were assisting Nolan Dalton."

Nolan didn't miss the tone that Russell had used when he'd said his name. There was definitely no love lost between them, but Nolan put that squarely on

Russell's shoulders. They'd butted heads when Russell had stonewalled him while Nolan tried questioning one of Russell's longtime clients. Russell had backed down, eventually, but that was only after Nolan had threatened to have him charged with obstruction of justice.

"Nolan and his partner are heading up the investigation," Adalyn said, her voice cool and clipped. "And I can't get into this now. I'll call you when I can."

"Your name is all over the news," Russell fired back. "That means Secure Point is on the news. Did Nolan drag you into this to smear mud on Secure Point?" But he didn't wait for an answer. "Because if he did—"

"No," Adalyn interrupted. "In fact, Nolan didn't drag me into it, and like I said, I can't get into this now." This time she clicked the end-call button, and she didn't answer when Russell immediately called her back.

"Sorry about that," she muttered to Nolan.

When she handed him back his phone, Nolan started to pull up one of the news sites, but Cody had beat him to it.

Cody cursed. "The Grave Digger is making a spectacle of this."

Yeah, he was. A spectacle that was obviously causing Caroline some serious flashbacks because she cried out when she saw the footage of her being dragged out of the grave. Jeb pulled her to him, pressing her face against his chest.

"The film came from the camera that blew up?" Jeb asked.

Nolan couldn't be positive of that since the Grave Digger could have had several cameras out there, but the angle sure looked right. "Probably," Nolan answered.

He continued to watch the footage, and it abruptly stopped right before Jeb had hurried onto the scene. Nolan was actually thankful for that. There'd be enough questions about why Adalyn was there. No need to add even more questions about Jeb. Especially if someone in the media picked up on the claim that Jeb was saying Nolan was his son.

Cody's gaze met Nolan's again in the mirror, and he took a deep breath before he shifted his attention to Jeb. "I hate to bring this up, but we need to consider if the Grave Digger isn't just connected to you and your long-lost son. But that he might be your son," Cody spelled out.

Nolan groaned, even though he'd already considered that possibility. Obviously though, neither Jeb nor Caroline had, and the shock of hearing that theory showed on their faces.

"No," Jeb immediately said while he shook his head. Caroline echoed his response.

Their denial, however, didn't stop Cody from continuing. "Your son would match the profile. White male between thirty and fifty," he provided. "And you don't know what kind of life he's had since he was taken. It would also explain why he brought Caroline and you into this."

Now, it was Adalyn who groaned. "None of the

other Grave Digger's kills had anything to do with Sheriff Mercer."

"Not that we know of," Cody quickly argued. "We don't know who he is or why he's killing. Heck, maybe those were practice. Maybe—" He stopped, probably because he realized this was a conversation that he should be having in private with Nolan.

But Cody's speculations had already hit the mark, and Nolan didn't think it was his imagination that Jeb and Caroline had both gone very pale. They were also quiet, no doubt mulling over the soul-crushing possibility of what Cody had said. Because if Joe Mercer had indeed turned killer, it likely meant he'd had a hellish life after he'd been taken from his family.

Nolan certainly didn't wish that on Joe Mercer, but he was a little bit thankful that the focus wasn't on the possibility of him being Jeb's son. However, there was another theory Nolan could add to the mix.

"Maybe this is all a ruse, a sick game being played by a mean SOB who wants to disrupt lives," Nolan laid out. "The Grave Digger could be just taking stabs at still-painful wounds."

Nolan believed at least parts of that were possible. But the part that didn't fit was Adalyn. Because it was no coincidence that the other victims looked so much like her. Other than Caroline, that is. And that meant either she was the motive, or Nolan was and that the killer would use Adalyn to get back at him in some way. Perhaps just a deadly game of cat and mouse.

Perhaps something more.

He needed to figure out what that was very soon

because he sure as hell didn't want to be running through the woods to try to get to her before she died. Unfortunately, the image of him doing just that was already way too clear in his head.

"You'll stay at my place until this is over," Nolan heard himself mutter.

Adalyn heard it, too, and her gaze slid to his. What she didn't do was jump to agree to that even though she'd been on board with the idea earlier. Nolan was ready to launch into the mode of convincing her to stay on board when his phone dinged with an incoming text. Because Nolan was watching her, he saw the muscles tighten in her face when she looked at the screen.

"It's from the Grave Digger," she said, and even though she'd kept her voice at a barely audible whisper, Cody practically sprang forward so he could see over the front seat. Nolan held the phone so that all three of them could see it.

Or rather all four.

Jeb moved in, too.

Hi, Adalyn, it's me, the text read. Did you enjoy seeing yourself on TV? You probably weren't looking your best, but it must have been fun to be reunited with your old flame, Nolan. Or is he still holding a grudge because of what happened? Yeah, I'm betting a grudge.

Nolan mentally cursed, and he made another sweeping glance around them. He wouldn't put it past the Grave Digger to use this as a diversion.

Who are you? Nolan texted back.

Don't bother trying to get me to chat. No time.

This has to be quick because I have places to go, people to see, he taunted.

Hell. Did that mean he was going after another victim right now? Nolan kept looking around the parking lot, kept hoping he'd catch a glimpse of him. And maybe he had. There were onlookers standing on the block just up from the hospital that had just been evacuated. At least a dozen people huddled together and were pointing at the building. Nolan took several videos of the group and would have the ERT enlarge and enhance them. It was a long shot, but they might get something. Of course, the killer wasn't just going to be wearing a sign announcing that he was the Grave Digger.

Adalyn took his phone and fired off a text before Nolan could stop her. You could meet with me, Adalyn responded, causing Nolan to curse. He didn't want her even hinting at the possibility of being bait. It's obvious you've got things to say to me.

No reaction. Not for several long moments. Then, the text came through.

I know you're looking for answers, the killer texted, and I'll tell you where to find them. You'll need to pay your old friend Donny Ray a little visit. Warning though. Neither you nor Nolan will care much for what he has to say because he's going to tell you bunches and bunches about who Nolan really is.

Chapter Six

Adalyn kept watch around them as Nolan exited the parking lot at FBI headquarters in San Antonio. Watched, while every word of the killer's texts sped through her mind.

Part of her wanted to shut it all out. To shut him out. But she couldn't bury her head in the sand. She had to face the threat and the past head-on.

That meant facing Donny Ray.

Some people might actually relish the notion of confronting the person who'd destroyed lives. But not Adalyn. Donny Ray would likely just use this visit as a way to remind her that she was the reason Nolan's father was dead.

Not that she needed such a reminder.

She lived with the horrible memories of it every single moment, but no way would Donny Ray miss an opportunity to shove the knife in a little deeper. And this particular knife would end up hurting Nolan. No doubt about it. His wounds were even deeper than her own.

"You don't have to go to the prison tomorrow," Nolan said, pulling her out of her thoughts.

It wasn't the first time he'd offered her alternatives since she'd gotten those texts. In fact, Nolan had said several variations of that in between making security arrangements for Caroline and dealing with the aftermath of the bomb scare. There'd been no bomb at the hospital; that was the good news, but it was a disruption the killer might try again—with real explosives and not just threats.

"I need to hear what Donny Ray has to say," Adalyn told Nolan.

That was a repeat, too, but obviously Nolan was hoping she'd change her mind and stay in protective custody while he made the trip first thing in the morning. He'd pressed for the visit to happen sooner, but the paperwork was still being processed. Added to that, it was already past 8:00 p.m. What with making the arrangements and both of them getting their cuts treated, the time had been eaten away, and it was a two-hour drive just to get to the prison. It was best to be fresh when facing down someone like Donny Ray.

"Besides," she added a moment later, "Donny Ray might not even talk to you. I was his target, not you."

No way could Nolan deny that, but it was obvious from the set of his jaw that he didn't like it. *Welcome to the club.* There were so many pieces of this puzzle of an investigation that she didn't like. Such as going to Nolan's house. But that's exactly where she was heading.

Where she'd spend the night.

Adalyn still wasn't sure that was the right thing for her to do since it'd be playing with fire, what with the old, and now reemerging, heat between them. But she was too tired to work out other arrangements. Besides, if Nolan didn't have to pick her up elsewhere, that meant they could get on the road even sooner for their trip to the prison. She wanted to get there and hopefully find out if he had a connection to any of what was happening.

"Donny Ray might not talk to either of us," Nolan argued.

She made a sound of agreement. That was true. But Adalyn thought it would be too tempting for the man to pass up. He'd want to see the damage he'd caused her, and this would be the perfect opportunity for him to do that.

"And even if he does talk," she added, "he might not know anything. The Grave Digger could be sending us on a wild-goose chase."

His sound of agreement had more of a growl to it, and she knew why. A wild-goose chase could be a setup to try to kill them, especially since the explosion hadn't managed to do that. But Adalyn had the sickening feeling that the Grave Digger wanted to play with them a while longer. Maybe play with Jeb and Caroline, too. Still, that didn't mean his endgame wasn't to kill them all.

For now, Caroline was tucked safely away. She'd need to be in the hospital at least for one night, maybe longer, but there would be guards posted outside her door at all times. Added to that, Jeb would be staying with her though Adalyn had seen the man was torn about going to the prison. Jeb was probably holding out hope that Donny Ray could give them the answers they desperately needed.

Answers that might tear Nolan to pieces.

Well, they would if the Grave Digger was right about Donny Ray having any actual info about Nolan. But Adalyn wasn't holding her breath. This could just be another way of playing with them. If so, it was working. She could practically feel the worry coming off Nolan. Worry that he might indeed be Jeb's kidnapped son. Adalyn didn't want to think what that would do to him if it turned out to be true. For now though, she pushed it aside. There was already too much to process.

Nolan took the turn toward his house, which was just on the outskirts of San Antonio. She'd been there before, of course. When they'd still been lovers. But right before their breakup and his father's murder, Nolan had talked about moving back to the ranch where he'd been raised.

His father's ranch. And the place the man had been gunned down.

Since there was another house already on the grounds and was only a half hour from San Antonio, it would be a doable commute to FBI headquarters, and Nolan had said he wanted to get back to something he loved—raising horses. Considering he hadn't made that move, Adalyn suspected the ranch held too many painful memories for him. Still, she hadn't heard of him selling the place so maybe one day he'd be able to call it home again.

He pulled into the long driveway that led to the

white-limestone-and-wood-frame house. It was surrounded by trees and shrubs. Not by neighbors though. This was a five acre lot, and while his nearest neighbor's house was visible, it was obvious that Nolan preferred the country feel of the place. So did she. Then again she, too, had been raised on a ranch.

"Hold off on getting out," Nolan instructed, and he used his remote to open the garage door. The moment he pulled inside, he shut the door and glanced around. No doubt looking for signs that anyone was hiding in there.

"You still have a security system, right?" she asked.

He nodded, showed her the app on his phone. "If someone had gotten in, I should have been alerted."

She heard the *should* loud and clear. Security systems could be tampered with or jammed, and while they didn't know if the Grave Digger had that particular skill set, it was best not to take any chances. That's why they both drew their guns when he finally gave the go-ahead to get out of the SUV.

He used his security app to unlock the door that led from the garage into the house, and they paused in the small mudroom, where he immediately reset the alarm. They also listened for any indication there was someone inside.

Nothing.

Still, they didn't let down their guard. Moving together and with their guns ready, they went through the house. It wasn't a huge place, but they were thorough, going through rooms that brought back plenty of memories for Adalyn. Especially Nolan's bedroom.

Mercy, she didn't want this attraction. But it was there, and she had to wonder if it'd ever go away.

"There's sandwich stuff in the fridge if you're hungry," he offered when they made their way back to the kitchen. He turned off the overhead lights, probably because he didn't want anyone outside to see them from the windows, but there was still plenty of illumination from the moonlight.

Before Adalyn could tell him that she wasn't the least bit hungry, his phone rang. "It's Megan Dailey from the ERT," Nolan relayed to her.

She recognized the name, mainly because Nolan had already made several calls to her and other ERT members to get updates.

Nolan answered the call and immediately said, "I'm putting you on speaker. Adalyn's here with me."

He'd no doubt told Megan that so she wouldn't spill anything that was supposed to be kept within FBI parameters, but at the moment, Adalyn didn't consider there was anything about this investigation she shouldn't be made aware of. The Grave Digger had put her right smack dab in the middle of it.

"Just wanted you to know that we're still processing the crime scene," Megan said after a short pause, "and we've made arrangements to have someone take Adalyn's car to headquarters. I also went ahead and looked at those videos you took of the bystanders near the hospital during the bomb threat."

"Did you see anyone in the crowd who fit the profile of the Grave Digger?" Nolan asked.

"There were three white males in the right age

bracket. I'm running them through facial recognition right now to see if anything pops."

Good. Though it was possible the Grave Digger didn't have a police record. But they might get lucky. Plus, if they could get IDs on those three men, they could do background checks to see if there were any red flags that pointed to one of them being a killer.

"Some people in the group had their phones out," Megan went on, "but none of the males meeting the profile were texting."

Adalyn sighed because she'd gotten those texts from the Grave Digger while Nolan had been taking the videos. Of course, the killer could have just been keeping out of sight. But there was another possibility. One that could have put the Grave Digger on scene where he could have watched the chaos he created.

"Is there any way to check and see if the killer used a scheduler app to send me the texts?" Adalyn asked. "Because, thinking back, he didn't directly reply to anything that Nolan or I said."

"We can go through your phone records and look for that." Megan responded so quickly that it let Adalyn know this possibility was already on her radar. "But if he took steps to cover himself, he probably didn't leave a trail."

Oh, he would have definitely taken steps to cover himself, not only there but also at the crime scene in the woods.

"Anyway," Megan went on, but then she stopped. "Hey, I just got a facial recognition hit on one of the gawkers who's got a sheet for drug possession. Jeremy Waite, white male, fifty-three. Ring any bells?"

Adalyn groaned because it rang a huge bell, and she wanted to kick herself for not having looked at the videos herself. She'd been so wrapped up in the aftermath of the attack, she hadn't remembered to do it.

"Jeremy is good friends with Donny Ray Carver," she explained. *"Good friends,"* Adalyn emphasized. "He claimed Donny Ray was with him when an elderly woman was murdered. A woman who'd hired Donny Ray as a handyman, and he robbed and killed her. I was closing in to arrest him—"

Now, it was Adalyn who stopped. No need to fill in the rest of that or to spell out that she hadn't closed in nearly fast enough because Donny Ray had managed to kill Nolan's dad. No need to spell out that she hadn't managed to get an arrest on Jeremy for giving a false statement, either, because he'd stuck to his story of claiming Donny Ray had been with him when the murder had been committed.

"His sister, Gillian, was involved with Donny Ray at the time of his arrest," Adalyn went on. "Check the video feed for a blonde woman in her early fifties, tall, athletic build."

"Give me a sec," Megan replied.

While they waited, Nolan went back to the videos to have a look for himself, and Adalyn watched as the feed moved on the screen. It didn't take her long to find exactly who she was looking for.

"She's there," Adalyn supplied. Gillian was standing several yards away from Jeremy, who was wearing a cowboy hat.

Nolan cursed. "It can't be a coincidence they're on the scene. I'll have them brought in for questioning."

"And I'll let you know if I get any other hits with facial recognition," Megan assured him before she ended the call.

Nolan put away his phone, and his gaze came back to her. Even in the dim moonlight, she had no trouble seeing the worry in his eyes. Maybe some relief, too. Because if the Grave Digger had "suggested" they talk to Donny Ray, then maybe this wasn't about Nolan's parentage. Perhaps it was because there was a connection between Donny Ray, Jeremy and Gillian.

And that had Adalyn shaking her head.

"If Donny Ray convinced either Jeremy or Gillian to be the Grave Digger, why would they serve themselves up to us on a silver platter by appearing on scene at the hospital?" she asked, talking just as much to herself as to Nolan. "And why wait now to pull me into it or point us to talking to Donny Ray if he's the one pulling the strings?"

"I don't know," he answered after a long pause, "but I intend to ask Jeremy and Gillian all of that. And more. Why don't you go ahead and get some rest, and I'll start the background runs on them?"

Adalyn gave him a flat look. "I'm not resting while you work."

"You're exhausted," he pointed out.

Yes, she was, but she had no doubt that he was just as tired as she was. Spent adrenaline could sap plenty of energy and make you feel bone-tired, and they'd both had a huge adrenaline spike what with the race to save Caroline and the explosion.

"We can start the background runs," she insisted. "Do you still have a desktop computer in your office?"

He nodded all the while giving her a considering stare. One where he was no doubt debating how to convince her to get that rest. Obviously, he gave up on that when he huffed. What he didn't give up on, however, was meeting her gaze, and in that gaze she saw the old memories stir inside him. Memories filled with heat.

The air changed between them, and she could have sworn it sizzled. Maybe though, that was just because her body was reacting to being so close to Nolan. Neither of them had time to do anything about the heated memories though because the slash of headlights coming from the front windows got their complete attention.

Both of them drew their weapons again.

Nolan moved fast, hurrying to the window, but Adalyn was right behind him. He took up position to the right of the glass. She took the left, and they peered around the jamb and into the yard just as a car pulled to a stop in front of the house. A vintage red Mustang that Adalyn immediately recognized. And she cursed.

"It's Russell," she muttered.

No need to explain to Nolan who that was. He knew it was Russell Mason, her boss. Russell and Nolan didn't exactly have a friendly track record with each other, and Nolan's sudden scowl reflected that.

"Why the hell is he here?" Nolan grumbled.

"He probably wants to see for himself that I'm all right," she answered on a sigh.

Still grumbling under his breath, Nolan disengaged the security alarm so he could open the front door. What he didn't do was put his gun away. Neither did Adalyn, not until Russell stepped out of the car and she saw that he was alone. After all, the Grave Digger or someone doing his bidding could have stolen the car and driven it here for another attack. But once Russell started toward them, she tucked her gun back into her holster.

Russell's stride wasn't exactly a peaceful stroll. No. He moved fast, and the anger and worry were there in his every step. He was tall, lanky and at the moment very pissed off.

"How'd you know I was here?" Adalyn asked.

"I went by your place, and you weren't there. Then, I went to FBI headquarters. They wouldn't tell me where you were, but when they said Nolan had already left work, I figured he'd taken you with him."

His tone was like his angry stride and body language. He definitely looked like a force to be reckoned with, and Adalyn knew there'd be some reckoning. However, that didn't stop her from continuing to keep watch around them, just as Nolan was also doing.

"I've been worried sick about you," Russell snarled, aiming a hard look at Adalyn before he glared at Nolan. She started to tell him that she hadn't had a phone, but Russell just rolled right over anything she would have said and jabbed his index finger in Nolan's direction. "You had no right to drag her into this investigation."

Adalyn's sigh got even louder. "Nolan didn't drag me into anything," she insisted just as Nolan snarled, "You have no right to be at my house and pointing that damn finger at me."

Russell lowered his finger, but his jaw stayed as set as steel. "You shouldn't have involved Adalyn in this," he spit out.

"Nolan didn't drag me into this," she repeated. "The Grave Digger did." She doubted Nolan would appreciate her telling Russell this, but she went ahead and added, "He sent me texts, leading me to his latest victim."

Russell volleyed glances between Nolan and her. Maybe he was processing what she'd just said or perhaps waiting for them to add more. "Why would the Grave Digger do that?" he asked when neither Nolan nor she said anything else.

"That's what I'm investigating," Nolan told him.

Apparently, that wasn't the answer Russell wanted because he huffed. "The Grave Digger dragged Adalyn into this because of you. Because you didn't back away from her. Do you know the hell she's been through? Do you even care that she's suffering because of what happened to your—"

"Enough," Adalyn snapped. The fury roared through her. Russell had a tendency to get overly involved in a lot of things, but he'd just crossed a very big line. "Nolan isn't the bad guy here. The Grave Digger is. And yes, he might have pulled me into the investigation because of my history with Nolan, but that's not Nolan's fault."

This time, Russell gave her a dose of his lethal glare, but it softened pretty fast, and just as fast, worry replaced the anger. "I remember how bad things were for you when you first started working for me."

No way could she deny that. She'd been a wreck, and if she hadn't needed a job, she might have just taken some time off to try to cope with the guilt that was eating her alive. Russell had seen that guilt. Had seen her break down a couple of times. And had gotten protective of her. She'd never wanted that from him back then and sure as heck didn't want it now.

"If you're a target of the Grave Digger," Russell continued, his attention still on Adalyn, "then I can keep you safe. You can stay with me."

"Adalyn's safe here," Nolan fired back. "She's in my protective custody."

Russell's eyes narrowed. "She'd be safer in mine. From what I can see, the Grave Digger wants to hurt you. Maybe even kill you. Adalyn could become collateral damage just by being around you."

She was well past the stage of possible collateral damage. The Grave Digger had seen to that by sending her those texts to lead her to Caroline.

"I'm okay, and I'll be safe here with Nolan," she assured her boss, looking straight at him so he'd see the determination in her eyes that was already in her voice. "I'm not fragile, and I'm not going to break into little pieces. What I am going to do is try to figure out how to stop the Grave Digger. I'll need time off to do that. I have vacation time coming, and I'll use that."

Adalyn braced herself for the arguments she figured Russell was already lining up. He could dispute that fragile claim, could also remind her that it wasn't her job to go after a killer. It was Nolan's. But Russell didn't say any of that. Instead, he took out his phone and handed it to her.

"I got those about a half hour ago," Russell said. "They came from an unknown account."

Adalyn focused on his phone screen and saw a picture of herself in the grocery store. And the icy chill snaked through her, head to toe. Because it didn't appear to be a grainy long-distance shot. It was clear, which probably meant the person who'd taken it had been close to her.

"You didn't know this was being taken?" Nolan asked, and Adalyn shook her head. Not exactly a stellar endorsement for someone in security not to have noticed something like that.

"There are more," Russell muttered. "Keep scrolling."

She steadied her fingers as best she could and went to the next photo. One of her jogging in the park near her house. Again, she hadn't known she was being photographed. Ditto for the third one of her getting into her car. In each of the three shots, she'd been wearing different clothes, which meant they'd been taken at different times.

Mercy, how long had this been going on? And how

had someone managed to get this close without her noticing them?

"The last one's been photoshopped," Russell said. There was a brace-yourself warning in his voice.

Adalyn took a deep breath and went to the shot. It hit her hard. Like a heavyweight's punch to the gut. Because it was a picture of her sleeping but instead of being in her bed where the photo had to have been taken, she was lying on the ground. Not actually *on* the ground though.

But in a shallow grave.

Chapter Seven

Nolan surrendered his gun at the first checkpoint at the prison and began to make his way through the security process. Behind him, Adalyn did the same, and he heard the little hitch in her breath that he totally understood. This breath hitch had nothing to do with the attraction between them or the nerves from just being here. No, it was about handing over her weapon when they were on their way to see a killer.

His father's killer.

It didn't matter that Donny Ray couldn't actually physically harm her today. Or kill again. But her body had to be firing off all kinds of signals that this was a primal sort of showdown with the person who'd tried to murder her and would almost certainly try again if he got the chance. And Donny Ray wouldn't care one bit who got in his way. That's why Nolan's father was dead.

No way could Nolan just push all of his feelings about that aside, but he was going to have to find some middle ground just to talk to Donny Ray. He reminded himself that something they could learn from the snake could save lives. Maybe Adalyn's and his lives. And while it was a long shot that Donny Ray would actually be able to help them catch the Grave Digger, it was a shot they still had to take. Too bad he wasn't taking it alone and that Adalyn was with him.

Before they'd left his house two hours earlier, Nolan had tried once again to convince her to stay put. Not alone, of course, but with another agent who'd be able to protect her. Adalyn had nixed the idea for the umpteenth time. Part of him was okay with that, simply because this way she would be in his sights. Another part of him though wished she didn't have to come out in the open while she was still a target.

Russell would have no doubt preferred that, too.

Even after Adalyn's insistence that she'd be staying with Nolan, Russell had continued to press, trying to get her to leave with him. Nolan had been on the verge of threatening to have Russell removed from the premises, but Adalyn had finally gotten through to him that she wasn't going to cave.

Nolan hoped that hadn't been a mistake.

Part of him was worrying that Adalyn might be in even more danger just by being around him. However, he didn't trust Russell enough with Adalyn's safety.

Adalyn and he made it through the next security checkpoint and then were led into the interview area where there'd be a glass divider between Donny Ray and them. Still, Nolan had no doubts that he'd be able to clearly see the killer's face. And he'd be able to see theirs. Since Donny Ray was as cocky as they came, he'd likely try to get a rise out of them. Nolan didn't want to give him even that much so he kept reminding himself not to fall for whatever crap the man tried to dish out.

"Maybe the lab will have something for us when we're done here," Adalyn muttered.

He made a sound of agreement but doubted she was just making conversation by bringing that up. Like him, her mind was on this interview but also on the fact that she was the Grave Digger's target. No doubts about that. Not after seeing the photos that Russell had brought to them the night before.

After Adalyn had come up with possible dates for when the photos might have been taken, Nolan had immediately sent the pictures to the lab for analysis, and since it was high priority, they might soon learn something useful.

At minimum, the techs could determine the position of the photographer in the first three shots. Since they'd been taken in public places, it was possible there were security cameras nearby that had captured the photographer. Or there could be witnesses who recalled someone taking pictures. Of course, it was possible the Grave Digger had hired someone to get those shots of Adalyn, but even a hired lackey could turn out to be a link.

The last photo, however, was an entirely different matter and would need a different kind of finessing by the techs. It might or might not have been taken in Adalyn's bedroom. Nolan was betting it wasn't. Since Adalyn worked in security, she no doubt had a decent system, one that she insisted she kept on whenever she was home as well as away. A breach of any kind should have set off the alarms, and according to her, she would have been alerted even if it'd been jammed or had malfunctioned.

It was possible the photographs had been taken through the window of her bedroom. Not exactly a comforting thought but better than someone having been in her house. It was equally possible that the photo had been manipulated to make it seem as if she was sleeping.

Or dead.

Of course, the Grave Digger had wanted Adalyn to feel that punch of fear over seeing herself as one of his victims. And the killer had succeeded. Nolan knew her well enough to have seen that it had shaken her to the core. Still, she was here, shoving all that aside so she could try to put an end to the killer's reign of terror.

Nolan was doing his damnedest to put an end to it, too. Cody and another FBI agent would be having a chat with Jeremy and Gillian today, to question them as to why they'd been at the hospital during the bomb scare. Nolan still intended to interview the siblings himself, but this would give him a head start since the entire morning would be tied up with this visit to the prison.

"I'm not sure it's a good idea for me to keep staying at your house," Adalyn muttered.

That snapped him out of his thoughts, and Nolan looked at her. That's all it took. One look. And he knew where this conversation was heading.

Yeah, he knew her well.

"If you can deal with Donny Ray," he said, trying to nip her objection in the bud, "you can deal with the fact you used to sleep in my bed."

The corner of her mouth quirked a little. "It's not the sleeping that's messing with my head."

He knew that, too. This was about the attraction. The same one that made him ache for her and had urged him to go to her the night before. But it was also about the Texas-size distraction the heat was causing.

"I just keep reminding myself that you'd regret it if we got involved again," she went on. "That you wouldn't be able to get past what happened with your father. That being with me would bring it all back for you."

All of that was possibly true. It seemed less true with her facing him right now. Of course, that again was the heat talking. Still, lust had a way of breaking down barriers even when the breaking would mean facing a past that would hurt like hell.

A side door opened behind the glass partition, and they automatically shifted their attention to the beefy dark-haired man who was being led toward them. Donny Ray might have been wearing chained restraints and an orange jumpsuit, but he still managed to pull off a carefree attitude.

Even though Donny Ray was sixty-six, he looked at least a decade younger, and he'd obviously managed to stay in shape. The only thing different about him was he had more gray hair than he had before he'd gotten locked up.

"Hell musta frozen over," Donny Ray joked, and he followed it up with a chuckle as he dropped down onto the seat. A position that put them at eye level with him.

Nolan had looked into the man's eyes before. He hadn't missed a single day of the trial and sentencing, and he'd made sure he didn't glance away or react when Donny Ray had tried to provoke him with the exact same smirk he was sporting now.

"You two here to arrest me for something else?" Donny Ray added, this time with a wink. One that he aimed at Adalyn. He then ran his tongue over his bottom lip in what Nolan supposed was meant to be a suggestive leer.

Adalyn gave Nolan's leg a squeeze, maybe because she thought he'd jump to respond to that. He didn't. Nolan went a different route by asking a direct question.

"Have you been in contact with your old pals Jeremy and Gillian Waite?" Nolan threw out there.

Judging from Donny Ray's quick blink, that wasn't a question he'd been expecting. "What about them?" Donny Ray countered.

Nolan shrugged. "I thought I was clear enough, but I guess not so I'll repeat myself. Have you been in contact with them?"

Donny Ray slid glances between Adalyn and him. No blink this time, but Nolan thought that was a puzzled expression on the man's face. Or else a fake puzzled expression.

"And before you lie," Nolan went on, "I'll get access to your visitors log. If you tell me you've had no contact with them, and I prove otherwise, then your lie would be obstruction of justice. I'll make sure that info is presented at your appeal trial."

It was an empty threat since there were no official charges against Jeremy and his sister. Still, the threat worked because Donny Ray nodded and then leaned back in his chair as if enjoying the sun at the beach.

"Yeah, I've had contact with them," Donny Ray said. "Nothing conjugal with Gillian though. Maybe you can see about fixing that for me. I sure miss being with a woman." And he went back to leering at Adalyn.

"Perhaps you should have considered that before you did something to get yourself locked away in a maximum security prison," Adalyn coolly remarked. "What kind of contact did you have with Jeremy and Gillian?" she added without even pausing. "And I'll give you another warning about lying. Remember that with the exception of your lawyer, all of your visits and conversations are recorded. Your correspondence would also have been monitored and read."

Because Nolan was watching Donny Ray, he could see the debate the man was having with himself as to what to say. Yes, the conversations would have indeed been recorded and letters and such would be monitored, but unless his old pals were arrested, none of it would factor into his appeal.

"They visited me," Donny Ray finally said. "Jeremy came once, and Gillian's come a couple of times. And that's the last question I answer until you tell me why the hell you're asking about them."

Nolan stared at Donny Ray. "They were at the scene of a crime and are now being questioned by the FBI."

Donny Ray cursed and shifted in the chair as if preparing to jump to his feet, but the quick movement of the guard had him staying put. Staying put while he clearly tried to rein in his temper. And his worry.

"Now, tell us why Gillian and Jeremy were there," Nolan insisted.

"So you can use whatever I say to arrest them," Donny Ray spit out.

"No, so I can figure out if there's any reason for their arrest," Nolan countered just as fast.

"There is no reason," the man snapped. He mumbled more of that raw profanity. "I told them to keep tabs on Adalyn for me, that's all. Tabs. Nothing more. So, you sure as heck better not be trying to set them up."

"Tabs?" Adalyn questioned, drawing Donny Ray's attention back to her.

"Yeah, tabs." No smirking and leering now. Anger was ruling his tone and expression. "I wanted to hear all about you moping around and boo-hooing. How you were scared of your own shadow and couldn't be a cop anymore. I wanted to hear every last detail of how you were suffering."

The anger was going through Donny Ray in hot thick waves now, and while none of this was fun for Adalyn to hear, her own expression never wavered. "You asked them to take pictures of me?" she pressed.

"No." Donny Ray's answer came sharp and fast.

"Remember that part about your visits being recorded," Nolan threw out there. "If you instructed them to take pictures, we'll find out."

"No," Donny Ray repeated, shifting his glare to Nolan. "It's possible they took some photos on their own, but if they did, that's on them, not me." He paused. "This is about that bomb threat yesterday. It's about how you two dug up that woman in the woods."

Donny Ray would have had access to the news so it didn't surprise Nolan that the man had heard about the bomb and had seen the footage leaked to the media. Since the man had brought up the subject, Nolan went with it.

"What do you know about the Grave Digger?" Nolan asked.

Donny Ray leaned close to the glass. "Not a damn thing, and you're not going to try to pin anything about him on me."

The denial was adamant and fast enough like his early "No" responses, but Nolan wasn't just going to accept that. "Well, he certainly seems to know you."

"Why do you think we're here?" Adalyn chimed in, picking up on Nolan's interview rhythm. "You think we wanted to make this drive because we missed you? Trust me, we didn't. And we didn't pick your name out of a hat."

Donny Ray shook his head, and his eyes widened. "That SOB said I had something to do with those murders? I didn't," he snarled. "I don't know him, and if he says different, then he's a liar."

"Why would he lie about something like that?" Nolan countered.

"To hell if I know. Maybe he likes to screw around with people. Maybe screw around with the two of you," Donny Ray amended, and his protest came to a screeching halt.

"Yes," Adalyn calmly admitted. "Now, tell us what you know about the Grave Digger's latest victim, Caroline Edmondson, and her boss, former Sheriff Jeb Mercer."

"Lie," Nolan snarled, "and everybody at your appeal trial will hear about it."

Nolan waited for another of Donny Ray's denials. In his gut, he wanted that. Needed it, even. Needed any possible connection with Jeb, him, the killings and the past to go all away.

But that didn't happen.

"I knew Caroline and Jeb," Donny Ray finally said.

Hell. That meant Caroline had lied to them when they'd asked her about Donny Ray. Well, maybe it did. The woman had been shaken up so it was possible she simply didn't remember him.

Adalyn touched her fingers to the back of Nolan's hand, but like his, her expression didn't change. Nolan knew that because if there had been any changes, Donny Ray would have picked up on it and tossed Nolan's pain right back in his face. Instead, the man groaned.

"Look, this doesn't have squat to do with anything," Donny Ray went on. "What went on up in Lubbock County was a lifetime ago."

"What did go on there a lifetime ago?" Adalyn pressed.

Donny Ray cursed again, but this time there was some dread in the mix. "Jeb Mercer hates me, okay? I worked for him on his ranch, and I was hanging around Caroline at the time."

"Hanging around as in lovers?" Adalyn continued.

"Hell, yeah, lovers," Donny Ray snapped. "So what? Neither of us was married or anything."

The "So what" went back to Caroline's denial that she didn't know Donny Ray. But something occurred to Nolan. "You were using the name Donny Ray Carver then?" Because the man had used several aliases throughout the years.

Donny Ray lifted his shoulder. "I think I was going by Don Daughtry in those days. Daughtry was my stepdaddy's surname."

Nolan bit off the groan that nearly escaped his throat. Maybe Caroline hadn't lied after all, and that meant he'd need to reinterview her.

"Anyway, Jeb accused me of stealing some saddles from the tack room," Donny Ray added. "The SOB was gonna arrest me, even when I told him I hadn't done it. It caused a big blowup, and I quit."

Nolan was very familiar with all of Donny Ray's arrests, and there hadn't been one in Lubbock County. Maybe because the man had left before Jeb could take him into custody.

"When did all of this happen?" he asked.

Donny Ray certainly didn't shrug this time. He seemed to freeze, and Nolan wished he had ESP so he could know what the hell was going on in the man's head. Nothing good, that's for sure because Donny Ray was studying him as if seeing him for the first time.

Studying him and looking for any resemblance to Jeb, maybe. Or maybe Nolan was just reading too much into it. Donny Ray wouldn't have known about a possible connection between Jeb and him.

Or rather he *shouldn't* have known.

The silence dragged on for several long moments, and Nolan just waited for the man to continue. That was better than trusting his voice right now. No way did he want to let this arrogant slime know that the mere possibility of being Jeb's son was tearing him to pieces.

"I think I've said enough," Donny Ray muttered, and he got to his feet. "I won't talk to you again unless my lawyer's with me."

Nolan watched as the man walked away, but Donny Ray cast one last glance at him from over his shoulder. Not a smirk, not this time. But rather worry. And it was the worry that caused Nolan's stomach to tighten into a hard knot.

"We can show Caroline his photo," Adalyn said, standing. She stayed right next to Nolan as he also stood, and she met his gaze. "Think it through," she muttered. "This could be just another piece of the game the Grave Digger's playing. He's obsessed with us, and he would have dug into anything he could use to try to torment us."

Nolan wanted to hold on to that. That this was all

just part of the obsession, like the photos of Adalyn the Grave Digger had sent to her boss. But obsessions had a start. A trigger. And he could no longer dismiss that the trigger had been pulled way back when Jeb's son had been taken.

With that weighing like stones on his mind, they made their way back through security, and once they were outside, Nolan fired off a text to get the process started for him to have access to all of Donny Ray's correspondence and his visitors logs. He needed to find out everything that had been going on in Donny Ray's life for at least the past year. Because if Donny Ray hadn't hired someone to kill Adalyn, then he, too, had become the Grave Digger's obsession since the Grave Digger had put that message on Caroline's hands.

"Donny Ray could be using the money he stole from the elderly woman he killed to pay for a hired killer," Adalyn suggested. "We never recouped those funds, and he could have hidden them away."

Since Adalyn had talked plenty about that investigation, Nolan knew those missing funds weren't a paltry amount but rather close to a quarter of a million. Plenty of cash to hire people to do his bidding.

Nolan glanced up at the darkening sky when they went outside. *Great.* A storm was moving in, and it would likely slow them down. Not good. Because right now, he wanted to get back to San Antonio and talk to Caroline. After that, Jeremy and Gillian were on his to-do list.

The rain began to smack against the windshield

before Nolan even pulled out of the parking area, and he hadn't made it even a half mile before they were in a downpour. He cranked up the wipers to full blast just as his phone rang.

He didn't recognize the number, but figuring it might be someone connected to the investigation, or the Grave Digger, he answered it anyway and put the call on speaker. However, it was a familiar voice that poured through the SUV.

"It's me, Jeb," the caller said. "We got a problem. Somebody managed to get a vehicle with explosives close enough to the hospital, and it just went off."

Hell. Not this, not now. Even over the pounding rain on the SUV, Nolan heard shouts, sobs and the sounds of chaos.

"How bad?" Nolan asked.

"I'm not sure. The blast rocked the building so there's likely damage, but Caroline wasn't hurt. Not physically. She's a mess right now though. That's her crying," Jeb supplied when there was another loud wail. "They're planning to evacuate her to another hospital, but my gut says to get Caroline to someplace where I know she'll be safe. I'm not asking your permission. I'm just telling you what I'm about to do."

"Let me make some calls," Nolan insisted. Because his gut was telling him the same thing, that Caroline was in danger. "I can make arrangements for a safe house."

"I'll call you when I can," Jeb said, talking right over him. And with that, the man hung up.

Cursing, Nolan hit redial to call Jeb back, but the

moment he did that, the sound thundered through the SUV. Not from the storm. No, this had come from beneath the vehicle.

Someone or something had set off an explosive.

Chapter Eight

Adalyn heard the sound, the thick thudding blast, a split second before Nolan's SUV jolted and then suddenly jerked to the left. Her heart went straight to her throat, and the adrenaline slammed through her. Her mind instantly registered they were in serious trouble.

Cursing, he tried to maneuver the steering wheel, but it seemed to be locked in place. "The tires blew out," Nolan snapped while he continued to grapple to regain control.

That was the thudding sound she'd heard, but it'd been much too loud for only one tire. It'd been more like gunshots. Probably from an explosive device like the one that'd been on the camera in the woods. Which meant this was likely the work of the Grave Digger.

Another attempt to kill them.

There was nothing she could do except brace herself. And pray. If they wrecked, both Nolan and she could die. So could others who just happened to be traveling this way and were unlucky enough to become collateral damage for the Grave Digger.

With the rain-slick roads, the SUV went into a skid,

and from the corner of her eye, she saw the other vehicles trying to dodge them. Horns honked, headlights flashed. There was the screaming shriek of brakes and tires, seemingly dozens of them, squealing on the slick asphalt.

This was a highway, a normally busy one, and with Nolan having no control, someone could crash right into them. Or vice versa. Either way, it would be almost impossible to avoid being hit.

The skid skewed the SUV into the passing lane, but Nolan continued to fight to gain control. It was a fight he was losing though because the blowouts and the rain had done their jobs.

She heard another loud sound. Not a blast this time. But metal ramming into metal. A blue truck had careened into the back of the SUV. Not a head-on crash, but it was more than enough to accelerate the SUV's skid and send them farther into the passing lane.

The rain had fogged up the side windows, and even with the defroster on, the back windshield was cloudy, but Adalyn still managed to see something that had her chest tightening like a vise.

A semi barreling toward them.

The truck driver's horn blared out in quick warning bursts, but there was nothing Nolan could do to get out of his way.

"Hold on," Nolan told her.

There was no panic in his voice, but there was something else. Hard, cold anger. Something she totally understood. The Grave Digger was risking dozens of lives, including theirs, so he could play this sick game. Worse, they might never know why they were his targets, but if they survived, it would make her only more resolved to find out why the heck he was doing this.

Nolan muttered his "Hold on" again just as the SUV skidded out of the passing lane and onto the shoulder. There was plenty of water here, too, and the rocks and debris that'd collected there slammed into the undercarriage of the SUV. Along with the horns, tires and brakes, it sounded as if they were in a fierce battle.

His phone dinged with a text message, one that Nolan obviously ignored, but she had a flash thought about Caroline and Jeb. About them trying to escape from the bombed hospital. And it made her wonder if the Grave Digger had set some kind of explosive for them, too.

Adalyn managed to get a glimpse out of the driver's side window, and her heart dropped again. There was a median dividing the four lanes of the road, but this was no grassy, flat area. There were trees, lots of them, and if they somehow managed to avoid those, then they could maybe end up on the other side to face oncoming traffic.

Everything seemed to happen in a blink. There was no time for her to think or react before the SUV slammed headfirst into one of the trees.

The airbags deployed, bursting out from the dash and smacking into them. Adalyn felt the seat belt clinch and vise against her just as the crash caused her body to whiplash forward. She felt the pain from every one of the cuts and bruises she'd gotten from the previous explosion, and the impact robbed her of her breath. Still, with all of that going on, she managed to realize one very important thing.

The SUV had finally stopped.

Around them, there were still the sounds of chaos, and there were now some shouts added to the mix. But she could hear those shouts, those sounds, and she knew by some miracle she was still alive.

But was Nolan?

That one question slammed into her as hard as the impact from the collision, and Adalyn forced her arms to move so she could bat away the airbag to get a glimpse of him. Some of the tension in her muscles eased up when she heard him doing the same. She kept batting, kept fighting, and she finally managed to see him.

Alive.

Thank God. Nolan was alive.

Like her, he was covered with the talc from the airbags, and he had some fresh nicks on his face. Would probably have new bruises, too. Maybe, just maybe, that would be the worst of it and he wouldn't have serious injuries.

She reached for her gun when someone yanked open her door, and she saw Nolan do the same. In that snap, she readied herself to fight a killer. But it wasn't the Grave Digger who'd opened the door. It was a woman in her twenties.

"Are you okay?" the woman blurted out.

No, she wasn't. She was shaken to the core and

would have new nightmares to go with the ones she'd been having for months, but she nodded in response to this Good Samaritan who was obviously trying to help. Despite the pouring rain, the woman had her phone out and was calling for an ambulance.

"Is anyone else hurt?" Nolan asked, glancing around.

Now that her door was open, Adalyn could see a few accidents. Fender benders from the look of it. She hoped there was nothing worse. Nothing like the SUV. The front end of it was practically wrapped around the tree.

Nolan opened his door, and pushing aside the airbag, he looked around. Probably to determine the damage, but considering he put his hand on the gun in his holster, he was also bracing in case there was another attack. One meant to finish them off right here, right now.

"Do you see him?" Adalyn asked. "Is he here?" It didn't matter that neither of them actually knew what the Grave Digger looked like because Nolan would be looking for someone who matched the profile.

His phone dinged again, and he managed to lift it and glance at the screen. When he cursed, she knew who it was from. Even though she winced from the pressure it put on her bruises, Adalyn leaned in and read the message.

Wasn't that fun? You think old Jeb and Caroline are having as much fun as you are? See you both real soon.

NOLAN SHUT OFF the firestorm of thoughts whirling in his head and focused on getting Adalyn and him safely inside his house. As a security precaution, he'd already had a bomb squad scan the perimeter of the house for explosives.

Thankfully, they'd found nothing.

And according to his security app, there'd been no indications of tampering or a break-in while they'd been gone, but Nolan didn't want to take any chances of the app being wrong. That's why he repeated the steps he'd taken the night before when he'd brought Adalyn to his place.

He pulled into his garage in the loaner SUV he'd gotten from an FBI field office, and he immediately lowered the garage door. He took a moment to listen, to look for any signs of trouble.

None.

Well, unless he counted that look in Adalyn's eyes, where he saw plenty of worry. No surprise about that. He was worried, too. They'd come damn close to dying, again, and it had taken a big emotional toll on her. Hell, on him as well.

And Caroline and Jeb.

Jeb still hadn't called Nolan to tell him where he'd taken Caroline, and the man wasn't answering his blasted phone. Nolan knew that because he'd tried to call Jeb at least a half dozen times on the drive back to San Antonio. He had to hope that Jeb was as good of a lawman as his reputation claimed and that he'd managed to get the woman out of harm's way. It didn't help that they didn't know where harm's way actually was or wasn't.

Adalyn and he went through the same security drill once inside and checked the house. Again, they found nothing, but that still didn't ease the tension in his shoulders and gut. It felt as if every one of his muscles had turned to stone. It'd definitely be a while before he could let down his guard. That wouldn't happen until he had the Grave Digger in custody.

"The doctor said you should take a hot bath to help loosen up your stiff muscles," Nolan reminded her.

That suggestion had come at the end of a lengthy exam where both of them had had confirmed that they had no serious injuries. That was something at least. But the doctor had also mentioned they'd be "plenty sore" from the whiplash. Nolan didn't have to wait for that to happen. The soreness was already there.

Adalyn made a sound of agreement, holstered her gun, but she didn't budge. The heavy sigh she made said it all. She was exhausted, spent and deeply worried. Nolan was on the same page she was, but he wouldn't give in to the worry and exhaustion. He intended to dive into the reports that had come in from the ERT who'd finished processing the crime scene in the woods.

"Why don't you take that bath while I fix something to eat?" Nolan added when she continued to stand there.

He wasn't the least bit hungry, but neither of them had eaten since breakfast and he wanted Adalyn to have a meal so she could maybe take the pain meds the doctor had given her. Of course, she probably wouldn't take the medication. He wouldn't, either, but Nolan was hoping she'd cave and get some relief from the aches she had to be feeling.

Adalyn finally moved, but she didn't go toward the guest room or bath. She turned and faced him. "I'm so sorry."

Nolan was sure he looked confused, because he was, but then he began to wrap his mind around the apology. Since she was apparently the Grave Digger's target, she was sorry that he'd been pulled into it.

"These attacks could all be aimed at me," Nolan pointed out. "I'm the one investigating him, and he could be trying to throw you at me as a distraction."

"If so, it's working," she muttered. Then, she groaned. "We're both distracted, and that's not going to get better."

Since Nolan didn't like lying to himself, he had to agree. In fact, it was probably going to get a whole lot worse. There were so many ways the Grave Digger could come at them. So many people he could target or kill just to play with them. And judging from the stark look in Adalyn's eyes, she was as well aware of that as he was.

Sighing, too, he reached out and pulled her into his arms for a hug. Yeah, it was a mistake. He was good at making those when it came to Adalyn, but damn it all to hell, he just needed her right now. Needed to feel her close to him like this. Needed the reminder they were both alive.

She looked up at him, and Nolan made another

mistake. He dipped his head and touched his mouth to hers. He might as well have stripped off her clothes and had sex with her because that was the kind of punch that little kiss packed. The heat from it slid right over the cuts, bruises, aches and tension. Like a soothing balm.

Oh, the memories came. Of course, they did. He'd kissed her plenty of times right here in this house, and those hadn't been mere touches of their lips. Those had been hard, hungry and foreplay that'd led them straight to the bedroom. Or wherever else they'd landed. That was exactly why he shouldn't deepen the kiss now.

But he did anyway.

Nolan slid his hand around the back of her neck, and mindful of her legion of bruises, he eased her to him. Eased into the kiss as well, but that's where the ease stopped. He had to taste her. Yeah, he needed that, too. Needed that familiar kick that sent his body revving. And revving is exactly what he did. He kissed her too long, too hard and too deep, and he kept on kissing her until he had no choice but to break away just so they could breathe.

Dragging in some much-needed air, Adalyn looked up at him again. Not with weary, troubled eyes this time. The heat was there. The need. Always the need. And he knew that familiar kick had sent her own body revving.

Nolan forced himself to take a step back. Then, had to force himself not to reach out for her again. "Sorry," he managed to say.

She nodded, pulled in another labored breath, nodded again. "Kissing me has to remind you of your father's murder."

He was sure he blinked. "It didn't while I was kissing you. I got a totally different reminder then."

It was probably something he should have kept to himself, but after everything they'd been through, it seemed stupid to hold back on that. Stupid, too, not to try to give her some peace of mind.

"I don't blame you for my father's death," Nolan told her, and while it was true, her thin smile told him that she wasn't quite buying it.

Adalyn patted his arm. "Maybe one day I'll be able not to blame myself."

The grief was right there at the surface and not a good combination with pain and fatigue. That's why Nolan reached for her again, but before he could pull her back into his arms, his phone rang. When he saw Cody's name on the screen, he knew it was a call he needed to take. Nolan had given Cody a brief update while Adalyn and he had been at the hospital near the prison, but Cody would no doubt want details. Nolan also wanted any updates Cody had managed to get.

"What the hell happened?" Cody immediately asked the moment he was on speaker. "Did someone at the prison tamper with your SUV?"

Good question, and it was one of those details that Nolan didn't have. "Don't know yet. But the lab guys already have the vehicle and are looking it over. I've also requested access to the security cameras in the parking area."

"I'll hurry that along for you," Cody offered. "How's Adalyn? How'd she hold up after seeing Donny Ray?"

"She did fine. She's here with me right now," Nolan added in case there was something that Cody wanted to hold back about the investigation.

"Good. I'm glad she didn't let that SOB get to her. What'd he have to say about the Grave Digger?"

"Not much," Nolan supplied, "but he admitted that he'd told Jeremy and Gillian to keep tabs on Adalyn."

Cody stayed quiet a moment. "Tabs," he repeated. "They're the ones who took those photos of her?"

"Maybe. Did Jeremy and Gillian say anything about that in the interview?"

Cody muttered some choice curse words. "The interviews didn't happen. They both lawyered up, and the lawyer is insisting we go to them at their office, rather than having them show up at FBI headquarters."

It wasn't unusual for people to make requests like that. Being on home turf lessened the stress. Of course, the FBI could *compel* the pair to come in, but that would involve some legal wrangling that took time. Since they weren't charging the couple with anything, not yet anyway, it was best to do the preliminary interview in the most convenient place for them. That might even make them more cooperative.

"I figure they lawyered up because they have something to hide," Cody tossed out there.

Maybe. Or maybe the siblings were aware that this

was a serious matter if they could be connected to the Grave Digger or the attacks on Adalyn and him.

"What time are the interviews?" Nolan asked.

"Ten and eleven in the morning. You'll be there?"

"Yeah." Though Nolan would have to work out some security for Adalyn. Or take her with him. She'd definitely want to hear what the siblings had to say, but he'd have to make sure it was safe to take her along. "Have you heard anything from Jeb Mercer?"

"No." Cody cursed again. "I want to charge him with obstruction of justice for this stunt he's pulling. He shouldn't have whisked Caroline away like that."

Probably not, but if Nolan had been in Jeb's boots, he might have done the same thing. That didn't mean Nolan liked what had happened. He would have preferred having a key witness in FBI custody and not with some retired cop gone rogue.

"Right now, I just want him to keep Caroline safe," Nolan said. "Let me know if you hear from him."

"Will do." Cody paused again. "Did Donny Ray happen to say anything about…well, you know, Jeb's missing son?"

Nolan had known he'd have to brief Cody on this, and it would go in his official report. Still, it wasn't an easy thing to get out. Because it was a connection that Nolan wished wasn't there.

"Donny Ray worked for Jeb about thirty years ago," Nolan explained. "He was also involved with Caroline."

"Holy hell," Cody mumbled on a rise of breath.

Yeah, that was a good way of putting it. "Donny Ray left Lubbock County after Jeb accused him of stealing."

"Wait, why didn't Caroline or Jeb tell us this when you asked her about Donny Ray?" Cody pressed.

"Because Donny Ray wasn't going by Carver back then. He was using the surname Daughtry."

Still, it bothered Nolan that Caroline hadn't at least mentioned that she'd once been involved with a man named Donny Ray or Don. Then again, it had been thirty years ago, and considering the bad blood between Jeb and the man, Caroline might not have wanted to bring it up in front of him.

"All right," Cody said as if gathering his thoughts. "What do you need me to do?"

"You can push to get Donny Ray's visitors logs and the security footage. I'm about to call the lab and see what they have."

"Okay, keep me posted," Cody answered, and he ended the call.

Nolan nearly jumped right in to contact the lab, but he looked at Adalyn. "If you go ahead and take that bath, I'll fill you in on anything I learn."

As he'd expected, she shook her head but motioned for him to follow her into the kitchen. "I'll make us some sandwiches while you talk to them. After that, we can argue about the pain meds that we already know neither one of us is going to take."

Nolan had to smile at that, and he went to the kitchen with her. He couldn't sit. He still had too much adrenaline coursing through him so he paced while he made the call and Adalyn began to gather the makings for sandwiches. It took him a couple of minutes to work his way through the lab personnel to get to the one who was working on his SUV.

"I haven't had a chance yet to reassemble the explosives," Alice Moran immediately told him. "But I know they were on a timer."

He took a moment to process that. Apparently so did Adalyn because her attention was nailed to him even as she opened the bread.

"I might be able to get a signature off the explosives," Alice went on, "and I can compare it to the one from the hospital in San Antonio."

A signature was a bomber's ID, and it meant Alice would be sifting through the minute particles to try to figure out the way the explosive had been constructed and the devices that'd been used.

"Right now, it's my guess that the explosives were rigged to two of your tires," the woman continued. "They weren't that powerful because there wasn't a lot of damage to the undercarriage. Essentially, they caused blowouts which in turn caused you to wreck."

Yeah, and by blowing out only two tires, it practically insured the SUV would go into a skid. Which it had.

"What about the timer?" Nolan asked. "Anything unique about it?"

"Maybe. I found some particles of dust embedded in it. Dust that doesn't appear to be matching the other debris from the explosion. *Appear*," she emphasized. "But it could mean the timer had been on the vehicle for a while. Days or even weeks."

Hell. Nolan had been hoping the device was placed on the SUV while it was in the parking area of the prison so they'd have footage of the person who'd done it. Now, they didn't even have a definite time-line, which meant it could have been put on while he was at the damn grocery store or a restaurant. Or even when he'd been in the woods digging Caroline out of the grave.

Nolan thanked Alice for that news he hadn't wanted to hear and told her to call him if she found out any-thing else. But for now, he was going to consider the explosives and the timer to be the longest in the al-ready long shots they had with this investigation.

Before Nolan could put his phone back in his pocket, it rang, and he saw Unknown Caller on the screen. Steeling himself up in case it was the Grave Digger, he took the call and put it on speaker.

"It's me," he heard Jeb say.

"It's about time," Nolan snarled. "Where the hell are you?"

"A hotel. Caroline's with me, and she's all right."

"What hotel?" Nolan pressed.

"One I'd rather keep to myself until I can figure out who I can trust."

Nolan didn't bother clamping down on the profan-ity he muttered. "And you can't trust me?"

Jeb wasn't quick to answer. "I believe I can, but

you're FBI, and that means you don't act solo. I'd rather Caroline's location not be leaked. That's why I'm using a burner phone because I didn't want it to be traced."

He didn't clamp down the groan, either. "If you tell me where you are, I'll arrange for a safe house. I'll do that," Nolan spelled out, "and keep everybody else out of the loop. I need to talk to Caroline about something I learned today. Something important."

"What?" Jeb asked.

Nolan dug in his heels. "I need to talk to her." He wanted to see the woman's face when he brought up her relationship with Donny Ray.

Again, Jeb paused. "I'll consider it, but for now I want to give you a heads-up about Russell Mason."

Adalyn was already paying close attention to the call, but that got her moving even closer. "He's my boss," she told Jeb.

"Yes, I know. He came to see Caroline after she was admitted to the hospital. He demanded to know if you were in the room with her. When I heard him yelling at the guard, I came out to talk to him. He thinks you're in danger and that I should step in to convince you to stay with him."

Adalyn sighed, shook her head. "I'm sorry—"

"No need to apologize. That's not why I'm calling about him. After he left, I got a bad feeling so I went to the window and looked out. Your boss was standing there on the sidewalk across the street. And he was looking directly at the building when the bomb went off."

Nolan saw Adalyn pull back her shoulders. No doubt bracing herself. Because Nolan doubted she was going to like what else Jeb had to say.

"I think you'd better take a hard look at Russell Mason," Jeb added a moment later, "because he might have had something to do with that explosion."

Chapter Nine

Adalyn knew one thing for certain. She wasn't going to be able to relax on this trip to interview Jeremy and Gillian. Not after what'd happened the day before on the drive back from the prison. Then again, she stood no chance of relaxing at any time until the Grave Digger was caught. This talk with Jeremy and Gillian might help with that.

Might.

It could turn out to be like the interview with Donny Ray where they'd gotten more new questions than answers, but Adalyn had to hope that the pieces of the investigation would soon fall into place. That included the pieces about her boss, Russell.

I think you'd better take a hard look at Russell Mason because he might have had something to do with that explosion.

After Jeb had told them that, Nolan and she had spent a good portion of the night going over every last detail about Russell and the attacks. She'd also spent a good portion trying to forget that mind-numbing kiss Nolan had given her. Hard to push something like that aside, especially since she'd spent a handful of hours in the guest room just up the hall from him.

The man certainly had a way of being unforgettable.

But that's exactly what she needed to do so she could focus on the drive and make sure the Grave Digger didn't have another go at trying to kill them. Her bruises and cuts were still fresh enough for her to know she couldn't let down her guard even for a second.

Nolan had personally swept the loaner SUV even though it'd been parked in his garage all night so that was one thing ticked off the security list. Both were also armed and kept watch of their surroundings. Added to that, Cody and another agent, Marsha Rawlings, were following them.

Jeremy and Gillian might not appreciate having three agents and a security specialist show up at their office, but it wasn't safe to go anywhere without backup. Even if the siblings weren't directly connected to the Grave Digger, it was possible they were on his radar. That meant they could either be the killers' tool or possible targets to further muddy the waters of this investigation.

Following the directions from the GPS, Nolan pulled into the small parking lot for Mother Nature's Landscaping and Lawn Service. The building itself was fairly small, probably less than a thousand square feet, but the grounds were filled in with what Adalyn supposed were examples of landscaping they provided. Some sections were bursting with flowers, while others sported water features. Still others had shrubs.

"I'll hang back," Agent Rawlings said. "I'll keep an eye on the vehicles."

Wise, considering the explosive that'd been put on Nolan's SUV. Wise, too, in case someone tried to come after them while they were inside.

"I might have to step out to take a call," Cody added as they walked toward the building. "After you told me about your call with Jeb, I requested a deep background check on Russell Mason. I know you're already looking into him, but I figured it wouldn't hurt to have three sets of eyes on it."

No, it wouldn't hurt, but it let her know that Cody thought there might be a problem with Russell, too. And maybe there was. Russell had certainly seemed, well, possessive or something when he'd come to Nolan's house to demand she leave with him. Still, she didn't want to believe he was involved with this. Because if he was, it meant she'd missed some signals about the man that she should have caught. It wasn't exactly a comforting thought to realize she might have been working with a criminal for all these months.

Nolan opened the front door of Mother Nature's, and obviously they were expected because the moment Nolan, Cody and she stepped in, Gillian was there to greet them. Not exactly a friendly greeting, but she muttered a hello and motioned for them to follow her around the reception counter and toward an office.

Adalyn knew the woman, of course. She'd inter-

viewed her several times when she'd been after Donny
Ray. Gillian had more or less cooperated in those interviews. Or rather she had given the appearance of
cooperation, but Adalyn had never forgotten that the
woman was romantically involved with Donny Ray.
That didn't make Gillian a guaranteed liar, but she
was a suspect. Still was.

Gillian led them into the office, which took up
more than half of the building, and along with a seat-
ing area, it had two desks. Jeremy was already sitting
on a floral green sofa with a man in his thirties who
immediately got to his feet.

"Tanner Carlyle," he said, making eye contact with
each of them as they introduced themselves. "I want
it on the record that my clients are fully cooperating
with this interview. Or at least they will as long as
they're not being railroaded."

Jeremy apparently found that funny because he
chuckled. Gillian kept up her steely stare as they all
took seats.

"I don't have railroading on the schedule today,"
Nolan snarled.

Jeremy laughed again. "Personally, I don't think
any of this is necessary, but my sister thought it'd be
a good idea if we had a lawyer here. You know, just
in case you change your mind about railroading."

"We just want the truth." Nolan kept his tone as
dry as West Texas dust. "Why were you at North Central Baptist Hospital day before yesterday?"

"We were looking for Adalyn," Gillian readily admitted. She guzzled some water from a bottle.

"Donny Ray asked us to keep an eye on her," Jeremy said, picking up the explanation, "so when we saw the story about the two of you on the news, we asked around and found which hospital you were at."

"Asked around?" Nolan snapped.

"Yeah, I've got a few EMT friends," Jeremy explained, and it reminded Adalyn of what Jeb said about not wanting to trust anyone. Leaks could and did happen. "I figured since you'd been hurt that we might get some pictures." He shifted his gaze to Adalyn. "Figured Donny Ray would like that since he hates your guts."

"The feeling's mutual," Adalyn assured the man, causing him to chuckle again.

"If Donny Ray asked you to keep tabs on Adalyn," Nolan said, drawing Jeremy's attention back to him, "he could have also asked somebody else to do his dirty work for him. And before you say anything," Nolan added when the lawyer opened his mouth, "know that I'll have access to Donny Ray's visitors log and the recorded conversations that went on during those visits."

"We're not doing dirty work for Donny Ray," Gillian snapped, her icy tone matching her glare. A glare she aimed at Adalyn. "Donny Ray was provoked into doing what he did. If you hadn't been pushing him so hard and wrongfully accusing him of murdering that woman, he wouldn't have snapped."

"That's one theory," Adalyn said. "An inaccurate one, but a theory."

Obviously, Gillian shared Donny Ray's hatred for

her, but before the woman got a chance to return verbal fire, the lawyer interrupted.

"My clients both visited inmate Donny Ray Carver on several occasions," he spelled out. "So, they'll be on the visitation logs, but neither of them engaged in any kind of criminal behavior. They simply went there to visit an old friend."

"And to get instructions about keeping an eye on Adalyn," Nolan added.

The lawyer huffed. "Not instructions. It was a request from Mr. Carver, that's all. An innocent request to keep abreast of a former cop who seemingly has a vendetta against him. Considering that Mr. Carver has now been pulled into an investigation involving a suspected serial killer, I think he had reason to be concerned."

"The FBI didn't pull *Mr. Carver* into the investigation," Cody spit out. "He was named as a person of interest and was interviewed."

"Named by whom?" the lawyer pressed.

Cody shrugged. "That info is privileged. And it's not why we're here. We need to find out if your clients are up to their eyeballs in not one but two attacks and whether or not they had any part in a recent kidnapping."

The lawyer's jaw tightened. "You're talking about the abduction of Caroline Edmondson." He took out some papers from a briefcase and handed them to Nolan. "My clients have ironclad alibis for the time of the woman's kidnapping."

Adalyn glanced at the lengthy report, which seemed

to be a blow-by-blow account of every hour for the times in question. Maybe it'd hold up when Nolan or Cody dug through it to verify. And they would indeed verify.

"I spied on you," Jeremy continued a moment later, "but that's it. Gillian and I have worked hard to build this business from scratch, and we wouldn't do anything to mess that up."

He sounded convincing, but since Gillian was still scowling, Adalyn had no idea if that was the truth. Maybe their ties with Donny Ray ran deep enough to do whatever he asked of them. Maybe even attempted murder.

"Tell me about Jeb Mercer," Nolan said, and because Adalyn was watching both Jeremy and Gillian, she saw the surprise go through their eyes. If it was a pretense, they both did a good job of it.

"I've heard Donny Ray mention him," Gillian admitted. "Why? Did something happen to him?"

Yes, Jeb had been dragged into the investigation when Caroline had been kidnapped and he'd gotten those texts from the Grave Digger.

"Did Donny Ray ever tell you to keep tabs on Jeb or Caroline Edmondson?" Nolan pressed, obviously ignoring Gillian's question.

"No," Gillian said after a long hesitation. Jeremy repeated that after his own pause.

"I've already given you my clients' alibis for the time of Miss Edmonson's kidnapping," the lawyer protested.

Nolan ignored him, too. "Did either of you take

photos of Adalyn?" he asked, glancing first at Gillian and then Jeremy.

"I did," Jeremy answered after having a whispered conversation with his lawyer.

A chill went through Adalyn. "When and where?" she demanded.

Jeremy shrugged. "Once when you were walking to your car. I'd planned to print it out and send it to Donny Ray, but I never got around to it."

Nolan jumped right on that. "That's all you took, just one photo?"

"Yeah. Why?"

Nolan shifted his attention to Gillian. "How about you? Did you ever photograph Adalyn?"

"No," she answered, and the woman didn't budge even under Nolan's intense stare.

Nolan nodded and abruptly got to his feet. "We'll be back in touch with you after I've listened to the conversations you had with Donny Ray on your visits to the prison."

It sounded like a threat. Maybe a hollow one since Adalyn wasn't positive Nolan would be able to get that kind of access until he had some proof of Donny Ray's participation in Caroline's kidnapping or with the Grave Digger. Still, even a hollow threat might be enough to get one of them to cave and admit they'd taken those photographs. If so, that could be a link to the Grave Digger. Of course, there was another possibility.

That either Jeremy or Gillian was the Grave Digger.

The profile had said the killer was a white male

between thirty and fifty, but profiles had been wrong before. Added to that, Gillian seemed strong enough to lift and put a drugged woman into a grave. Ditto for Jeremy.

"Why'd you cut the interview short?" Cody asked Nolan the moment they were outside.

"I wanted to give them something to think about." Nolan took out his phone, and she heard him request a tail be put on both Gillian and Jeremy. "I want to see where they go, what they do in the next twenty-four hours. They probably won't try to contact Donny Ray, but I'll check that out, too."

"I can do that," Cody volunteered, following them to their SUV.

Nolan hurried Adalyn inside the vehicle, but she didn't breathe easier until he was inside as well. The windows were bullet resistant, and even though the Grave Digger hadn't been known to shoot his victims, it was best not to take any chances.

"You think either Jeremy or Gillian could be involved in the attacks?" Adalyn came out and asked as Nolan drove away from Mother Nature's.

"I'm not sure. I keep thinking if they were, they would have better covered themselves, that they wouldn't have visited Donny Ray. That they would have wanted to keep their names off any visitors log." He paused, kept watch around them. "But it's possible they didn't come up with the plan until after their visits had started. No way to go back and undo the logs."

"True," Adalyn admitted. "But why wait all this time to pull me into it?"

"Maybe he just wanted you to know what you'd be facing when he brought you into this." Nolan's answer was fast enough to let her know he'd given this lots of thought. "The same for me," he added.

While Adalyn mulled that over, they drove back to Nolan's house, which wasn't far. Only a ten-minute drive, and along the way, Adalyn saw nothing out of the ordinary. She didn't let down her guard though because it was entirely possible that the Grave Digger could make things appear *ordinary*. That might be how he, or she, had managed to get to the victims.

Nolan parked in his garage, and once they'd taken their usual security steps, Nolan sent Cody a text to tell him it was okay, that he could leave. The moment he finished, his phone rang, and Unknown Caller popped up on the screen.

"It's me," Jeb said the moment Nolan answered the call. "I heard on the news about what happened yesterday to Adalyn and you. Are you both okay?"

"We're fine," Nolan snapped, indicating that nothing was actually fine. "I have to talk to Caroline."

"She's sleeping right now—"

"Let me rephrase that. I *will* talk to Caroline. I think I might know the reason she was kidnapped, but I'm not going to get into it over the phone. I need to see her. That's not a request, Sheriff Mercer. You'll tell me where you are, and I can arrange to have her brought to some place safe where I can question her."

"Question her?" Jeb repeated. "What's going on?"

"You'll find out when I've seen her." Nolan's voice was as hard as the set of his jaw. "Again, that's not a request. I'll unleash a statewide manhunt if you don't comply, and when you're found, I'll have both of you arrested."

Silence. For a long time. "All right," Jeb finally said. "I'll get her to you by this evening."

Nolan opened his mouth, no doubt to ask for details as to how Jeb would do that, but the man had already ended the call. Adalyn didn't have to ask Nolan if that statewide manhunt was a bogus threat. It wasn't. Right now, Caroline could be the key to critical information, along with being a possible target.

"Guess Jeb won't be so eager now to buy into the hogwash of me being his long-lost son," Nolan grumbled. But then winced and waved that off. "Sorry."

"No." She took hold of his arm, turning him to face her. "I wondered if that claim was bothering you. I mean, I know it was bothering you," Adalyn amended. "I just didn't know how you were processing it." Now, she groaned because that last part sounded so clinical, like something a counselor would say.

"I'm not processing it because it's not true." Nolan didn't groan after blurting that out. Not aloud anyway. "I have enough to worry about without dealing with what-ifs."

He looked at her with those amazing eyes that could make her feel as if she were drowning in all those shades of dreamy brown and amber. "I'm on your worry list," she said.

"Yeah," he admitted without even a breath of a pause. "For a lot of reasons."

"Two reasons," Adalyn corrected. "One because you're afraid you can't protect me." She did pause for a breath. "And two because you're thinking about having sex with me, and that's a distraction."

Nolan reached out and skimmed his thumb over her cheek. "Yeah," he repeated. "When this is done, when you're safe and the Grave Digger is behind bars or dead, then sex won't be a distraction. But maybe it'll be something else then. A complication."

That didn't sound good, like maybe he was pulling back from the memories of his father that were tangled up with her. But if so, that didn't stop Nolan from pulling her to him. No steamy kiss this time though. However, he did brush his mouth over the top of her head.

It still packed a punch.

Of course, the best punch came from his body being pressed against hers. Yes, sex was a distraction, but Adalyn figured so was just thinking about sex, something she couldn't shut off when she was near Nolan like this.

All thoughts of distraction and sex vanished when they heard the vehicle approaching the house. In a reflex move, Nolan pulled her behind him, drew his gun and went to the window. Drawing her own gun, Adalyn joined him there, and she watched as Cody stepped out of the car. The very car that Agent Rawlings and he had driven away in minutes earlier. Agent Rawlings was still behind the wheel, but she didn't get out as Cody hurried to the house.

Nolan disengaged the security system, opened

the door and Cody rushed in. He was holding up his phone.

"I found something," Cody announced. And while Nolan shut the door, Cody pulled up some photos on his phone.

Photos of Adalyn.

"These are the pictures that Russell said the Grave Digger sent to him." Cody's words rushed out, and Adalyn could tell he was excited. "The lab just got back to me on them, and here's what they found."

Cody enlarged one of the pictures of her shopping, and he tapped the large window directly behind her in the shot. When he kept expanding the picture, she saw the image of the man reflected in the glass. A man holding up his phone as if taking a picture.

And her heart went to her knees.

"Russell," she murmured.

Nolan looked at her, maybe to see how she was handling this or maybe to confirm that it was indeed Russell. Adalyn managed a nod. The shot was grainy, but she was almost positive that it was Russell.

She quickly went back through the date when it would have been taken. The day before the Grave Digger had sent her that first text about Caroline.

"I want to talk to him," Nolan snarled, taking out his own phone.

"Hold off," Cody advised him. "There's more." He shifted his attention to Adalyn. "And brace yourself because you're not going to like it."

She didn't like it already, but Adalyn could tell from Cody's expression that this was going to be very, very bad. "Is Russell the Grave Digger?" she came out and asked.

"You tell me after you hear what I've learned. First though, answer something for me. Did you seek out the job working for Russell, or did he come to you?"

That bad feeling got worse. "He came to me," Adalyn admitted after clearing her throat. "But I did a thorough check on his company, Secure Point. There were some red flags, such as Russell planting eaves-dropping equipment where he shouldn't have, but I told him I wouldn't be doing any of that. And as far as I know, he stopped doing it, too."

Or so she'd thought. But maybe he'd just gotten better at hiding it.

"I went through his background," Cody continued without taking his gaze off her. "Not only on Secure Point but on Russell himself. I dug deep. Did you know that thirty years ago, when he was in his twenties, that his fiancée took her own life?"

Adalyn had to shake her head. There'd been nothing about that in his bio, but that generally wasn't something that would be included. Especially since it'd happened so long ago.

"Russell was living in Lubbock County at the time," Cody said. "Living just miles from Jeb Mercer, who was in his heyday as sheriff. The very sheriff that had some run-ins with Russell's family. I'm guessing you didn't know that?" He aimed that question at both Nolan and her, and she had no trouble hearing the underlying accusation.

That maybe Russell wasn't just the Grave Digger

but that he was also the person responsible for taking Jeb's son.

"I hadn't heard about any of this," Adalyn muttered, and Nolan made a sound of agreement. She bit back telling him how sorry she was that she hadn't dug as deep as Cody obviously had. But later, she'd owe him a huge apology.

"Now, back to Russell's fiancée," Cody went on. "Her name was Kimberly Charles, and he walked in on her in bed with another man. There was a fight between the men, and during the scuffle, Kimberly grabbed a gun and shot Russell in the leg. He obviously didn't die, and after Mercer investigated, she ended up pleading down to misdemeanor domestic violence since she claimed the gun went off by accident."

"A light sentence," Nolan remarked. "How'd Russell take that?"

"Not well. Kimberly got only a few months in jail and ended up dying from suicide less than a year later. Russell left Lubbock County to move here."

Nolan shook his head. "I really need to talk to him," he repeated.

"And I want to be with you when you do," Adalyn insisted.

"Same here," Cody said, "and then you can hit him with this little fact. Other than Caroline, all the Grave Digger's victims have similar physical characteristics."

"They look like me," Adalyn muttered.

"No," Cody argued. "They look like *her*. And if

you're looking for a motive for the Grave Digger, look no further than here."

He pulled up another photo of a brown-haired woman with blue eyes. For Adalyn, it wasn't like seeing herself in a mirror, but she had to admit she shared a strong resemblance with the woman.

"That's Kimberly Charles," Cody said, tapping the woman's picture. "And I believe with every victim he kills, Russell is getting the justice he thinks he deserves."

Chapter Ten

Nolan was second-guessing himself about going to FBI headquarters with Adalyn, but he'd needed access to files that he couldn't get at home. And it was also where he wanted to question Russell. That had meant another trip outside, another chance for the Grave Digger to come at them.

But thankfully, that hadn't happened.

Since he couldn't legally give Adalyn access to the info he was diving into, Nolan was working alone at his desk, but she wasn't just sitting idly by. She was in the chair across from him and was using his personal laptop to do some unofficial diving into her boss's past. A past that Nolan figured was eating away at her right now.

With the red flags that Russell might be the Grave Digger, it meant Adalyn might have been working next to a killer for months. And worse, a killer that might have lured her into a job just so he could keep her close for his plan to kill her. It sickened Nolan to think Russell might have been able to get away with it. Since she worked for him, she likely wouldn't have hesitated to go somewhere with him if he'd asked. That somewhere could have been to a shallow grave when he finally intended to kill her.

Cody wasn't staying idle on this part of the investigation, either. He was at the prison doing battle to get Donny Ray's visitors logs and conversations released. Donny Ray's lawyer was fighting that, citing some legal babble about the conversations being misconstrued, which in turn could be prejudicial for his client's appeal. It wasn't a fight that Donny Ray would win, but he could delay things that shouldn't be delayed. Things that might help them catch a killer.

Nolan's phone dinged with a message he'd been waiting for—confirmation that Russell would indeed be coming in for an official interview at 3:00 p.m., which was only thirty minutes from now. It was fast work setting up the interview, especially since it'd been only a couple of hours since Cody had dropped the bombshell and shown them the photo of Russell's fiancée. Nolan would definitely question Russell about all of that, but he still needed to talk to Caroline and Jeb as well. If Jeb hadn't shown up as promised by tonight, Nolan would start the process to find him.

Unfortunately, it was a process the Grave Digger might be taking as well.

Such as trying to triangulate Jeb's location from the last calls he made before he'd started using a burner. Also tapping into his GPS data and any money trail Jeb might have left. Jeb had said he had Caroline at a hotel, and while he probably wouldn't have used his credit card to secure the room, phone calls and Internet searches could be made to see who'd used cash to check into nearby hotels. That kind of info would require a warrant, but Nolan had no doubts he could get one.

"Russell will be here in about thirty minutes," Nolan relayed to Adalyn. "Marsha Rawlings will do the interview."

Her head whipped up, her gaze snaring his. "I know I can't go into the room, but I want to observe."

Nolan nodded, but he gave her a bit more than that. "When Russell gets here, Marsha will alert me, and we'll both go out to *greet* him. I'm sure he'll want to talk to you. He'll be Mirandized by then so anything he says can be used against him."

"He's careful so he probably won't say anything incriminating. But he will be furious," Adalyn added. "Sometimes, angry people say things they shouldn't." She paused. "And just seeing me might trigger his anger even more."

That's what Nolan was counting on. Just because Adalyn wasn't FBI or a cop, it didn't mean he couldn't use her. He didn't especially want to see her facing down her boss, but he'd be right there with her in case things got ugly. He doubted Russell would resort to violence and do a flip and go into the Grave Digger mode, but Nolan could watch for clues that the man was the killer Cody believed he was.

Adalyn stood, pressing her hands to the small of her back, and Nolan didn't miss the wince she made. "Are you all right?" he asked.

"Just sore muscles."

He suspected there were some bruises adding to the discomfort as well. He sure as hell had plenty of them. The Grave Digger had certainly left his marks on them in more ways than one.

"How about you? Are you okay?" She tilted her head, stared at him, and he thought her question included a lot of things. Not just their injuries and the Grave Digger investigation but also this attraction that was going on between them.

Nolan was debating how to answer that when his phone dinged again, and he saw Marsha's text.

Russell's early. He just walked in, and surprise, surprise, he didn't bring a lawyer with him. I'll have read him the Miranda before he sees you.

He showed the screen to Adalyn and then got her moving toward the interview rooms, just as Marsha and he had discussed. They intercepted Russell and Marsha in the hall. As expected, Russell stopped, and he aimed vicious glares at both Adalyn and him.

"I'm not the Grave Digger," Russell spit out like profanity. His glare worsened when his attention shifted to Adalyn. "And you should know that. You should have told his rogue agent friend Cody Hill that you know I'm not capable of doing something like that."

"Kimberly Charles," was all Nolan said in response to the man's tirade.

Russell froze. For a moment anyway. And Nolan could practically see him mentally regrouping. When the regrouping was done, Russell's eyes went flat, and he huffed.

"That's what this is all about?" Russell snapped. "Agent Hill thinks because my fiancée screwed me over a lifetime ago that I've gone off the deep end and am killing her over and over again. Well, that's about as stupid of an accusation as stupid can get. And ask yourself why Agent Hill would say something like that. Why?" he emphasized in a snarl.

"Because it's a valid theory that gives you motivation," Nolan readily provided, but he had to wonder why Russell wasn't just digging in his heels on the denial instead of trying to turn this back on Cody.

"It's not valid," Russell insisted. "Think it through. If I'd wanted Adalyn dead, I could have killed her months ago. I'm not a killer." He paused, staring right into Nolan's eyes. "But Cody Hill might be."

Adalyn didn't groan or throw her hands up in the air, but Nolan thought that might be what she wanted to do. "Okay, I'll bite," she said. "Why would you think he's a killer?"

"Because I caught him on the camera that I set up outside your house, that's why." The moment the words left Russell's mouth, he froze again. Then, he muttered some profanity under his breath.

Adalyn froze, too, but it didn't last. "What do you mean the camera you set up outside my house?"

Russell ground out more of that profanity and took a deep breath. "You told me that you thought you were followed, and I was worried about you. So, I set up a camera in one of the trees in your yard."

"You set up a camera without telling me?" The anger came through loud and clear in her voice, and Adalyn was doing some glaring of her own.

"I just wanted to see if someone was lurking around, and I wanted to do that without alarming you. And someone was lurking. Agent Hill," Russell insisted.

Adalyn folded her arms over her chest. "You saw Cody Hill at my house?"

"Either him or someone who looks like him. But I'm betting it was him, and it's the reason he's trying to accuse me of being the Grave Digger. It throws suspicion off him."

"There is no suspicion on Agent Hill," Nolan reminded him.

"Well, there sure as hell should be. You could have a killer under your own nose."

"Yeah, we could." And Nolan looked straight at Russell when he said that.

Russell held his narrowed gaze on Nolan a moment longer before he shifted to Adalyn. "This is why it's so important that you let me protect you. Nolan's blind to the danger around him, which means he could end up getting you killed."

"I trust Nolan," Adalyn said, shaking her head. "And I want you to give him the footage from the camera that you illegally placed on my property. Footage that'll be examined to see who else other than you violated my privacy. If you don't turn it over, I'll press charges against you."

The shock went through Russell's eyes. Then, the

anger came. It returned with a vengeance. "I gave you a job. I looked out for you."

"Yes, but you crossed a very big line," Adalyn argued. "And you can consider this my thirty days' notice. I won't be working for you any longer because I quit."

She turned and walked away but not before Nolan heard Russell curse again and then tell Marsha that he wanted a lawyer. Nolan didn't blame Adalyn for putting the man's back up like that. Russell had indeed crossed that line between employer and employee. Marsha might not appreciate that Adalyn had gotten the man so riled, but Russell would have almost certainly played the lawyer card when he realized he was indeed a murder suspect.

Nolan followed Adalyn back to his office, and because she'd likely need a moment, he closed the door. She took that moment in his arms. She stepped right into the embrace he offered, and the sound she made was part sigh, part groan. Nolan was doing some mental groaning of his own over the bombshell Russell had dropped with his accusation at Cody. And with violating Adalyn's privacy. But, ironically, it was that violation that might give them some answers.

"Do you really think Cody could have been on the camera footage?" Adalyn muttered.

Nolan had already anticipated this question and was mulling it around. "Depends on when it was taken. It's possible he checked out your place after the Grave Digger dragged you into this. There were a lot of moving pieces involved in the aftermath of that."

"Yes," Adalyn said, easing back so she could meet his gaze. "Yes," she repeated, sounding relieved.

Nolan would be relieved, too, if it was true. "Let's find out."

He took out his phone, pressed Cody's number, but the call went straight to voice mail. He didn't read anything into that because it was possible Cody was still at the prison and had turned off his phone.

"If it's not Cody on the footage," Nolan added, "we might get our first look at the Grave Digger. Might," he emphasized. "Because if Russell is behind these murders, he wouldn't just hand us images of himself. He'd doctor the feed. But the lab would be able to tell if he'd done that."

"And it would mean he's at least guilty of obstruction of justice," Adalyn concluded.

That was true, and there could be even more charges if that image doctoring had been done to set up an FBI agent.

The knock on the door had Adalyn taking another step back, and he paused to gather himself before answering it. Marsha was standing there with a visitor.

Gillian.

Nolan definitely hadn't expected her to show up, and he found himself studying her while he wondered if she could be the Grave Digger. She certainly had a strong enough build for it, and she did have that connection with Donny Ray.

"I need to talk to you," Gillian immediately said, stepping into his office. The nerves were practically coming off her in waves.

Nolan made eye contact with Marsha to make sure Gillian had been checked for weapons, and the agent nodded. "You want me to put her in an interview room?"

"No, we can talk in here. Let me know what happens with Russell," he added in a murmur, and he shut the door.

"You didn't bring your lawyer with you?" Nolan asked Gillian, and he waited to see if she would object to Adalyn being there. She didn't.

"No. I have to tell you about Donny Ray," she blurted out. Then, paused. Then, she started to pace. Well, pace as much as she could, considering his office wasn't that big. "Donny Ray asked me to scare Adalyn, and we worked out a code of sorts before he was sentenced. If he said the word *bingo* during one of my visits to the prison, then I was supposed to start scaring her."

Adalyn stepped in front of the woman to force eye contact. "And how exactly were you supposed to do that?"

Gillian didn't have a defiant glare like Russell. Instead, Nolan saw guilt. Her shoulders drew up, and her chin dipped down. "Donny Ray left that up to me. So, I followed you a few times, and before all of this latest mess happened, I'd planned on sending you a threatening letter. You know, like one of those with letters cut out from magazines or something."

"That's it?" Nolan pressed after Adalyn and he exchanged a glance. "You didn't send her texts to lure her into the woods?"

"No," Gillian jumped to say. "I didn't do that. Wouldn't do that," she amended. "And neither would Jeremy. My brother doesn't know anything about this."

Nolan shrugged. "Maybe Donny Ray worked out a code with him, too. Maybe he wanted Jeremy to do more than just scare Adalyn."

Gillian was shaking her head before Nolan even finished. "Look, Jeremy can be irresponsible sometimes, but he's not a killer." She paused again. "Donny Ray is though."

Nolan clamped down on the surprise he felt. He definitely hadn't expected the woman to admit something like that. "You want to get into specifics about that?" Nolan asked, and depending on how she answered, he might be Mirandizing her and taking her in for an official interview. He was betting she'd be calling in her lawyer once he did that.

Gillian sighed, and using both hands, she pushed her hair from her face. "I mean, he killed your father, and no, I'm not getting into whether or not he killed that woman he was working for."

She probably didn't want to talk about that because it could end up incriminating her if she'd lied to give Donny Ray an alibi. Which Nolan was certain Gillian had done.

"I just don't want you to think my brother is like Donny Ray," Gillian went on. "He isn't."

Nolan did wonder exactly that, and he tried to figure out what Gillian had hoped to accomplish by coming here. Maybe it was some kind of reverse psychology?

A ploy so Nolan wouldn't think that her brother or she was a killer?

"I won't be visiting Donny Ray again," Gillian went on. "As far as I'm concerned, he's out of my life now."

With that, the woman went to the door and walked out. Nolan considered stopping her, but he doubted there was anything else she could tell him. Not that she'd actually told him anything, but he'd be giving a lot of thought as to what her visit might have been all about.

Gillian was still making her way back to the front reception area when he spotted Marsha coming from the interview rooms.

"Russell ended the interview," the agent told him. "When I asked him about his possible involvement with the Grave Digger murders, he said he'd come back in the morning with his lawyer."

Nolan didn't groan because it was exactly what he'd expected. Russell wasn't stupid, and he no doubt had a lawyer on retainer.

"I don't suppose you can hold him?" Adalyn asked.

"Not on anything to do with the murder," Marsha readily answered. "It's not enough that the victims look like his ex-fiancée, and a lawyer could argue there's no physical proof. Which there isn't. We could maybe hold him on putting up the camera on your property, but it'd be a misdemeanor."

That'd barely be a slap on the wrist. If Russell was the killer, Nolan wanted to be able to prove it.

"What about the footage from the camera he set up at Adalyn's?" Nolan asked.

Marsha gave him a thumbs-up. "He's agreed to turn that over to us before his interview tomorrow."

"Good. I want a copy of it," Nolan told her. "And, of course, I want it sent to the lab for priority processing."

"Will do. Say, why don't you go ahead and take Adalyn home?" Marsha asked after glancing at Adalyn. "You two look beat, and I can handle the paperwork on Russell. I can also text to have backup follow you. You have all the files you need?" she added, tipping her head to his computer.

Nolan did have the files that he could take with him, and he'd already read the ones that couldn't be downloaded to his computer. Still, he normally would have helped Marsha with the chore of the paperwork, but the truth was, he was beat, and Adalyn looked ready to drop.

"Thanks," he told Marsha, and taking her up on her offer, Nolan gathered his things.

Adalyn certainly didn't balk at leaving, and he hoped once he got her back to his place that he could talk her into taking a nap. Alone, of course. She needed rest, not sex. And he shut down his body's protest over that.

As Marsha had said, she'd texted for backup, so when Nolan pulled out of the parking lot so did two agents in an SUV. He knew them both. Knew, too, that he was going to owe a lot of people a huge thanks for adding to Adalyn's protection like this.

While he kept watch around them, he tried Cody again, and this time, he left a message to return his call at the first chance he got. Nolan didn't want to cut short anything Cody was doing at the prison, but he needed to talk to him. Needed to hear Cody either deny all of Russell's claims or have an explanation as to why he was at Adalyn's house.

An explanation that Nolan would carefully examine.

Because Russell was wrong about him being blinded to the possibility that a fellow agent was a killer. With Adalyn's and others' safety at stake, Nolan had no intention of overlooking anything that could lead them to the truth.

"I don't want to take a nap," Adalyn said, making him wonder if he was just that easy to read. "I don't want the nightmares."

Hell. He certainly hadn't forgotten about the dreams all of these attacks must have brought on, but sleep wasn't exactly an option. "You can't just keep pumping caffeine into your system."

"I know, but I'd like to put off sleep until it's actually nighttime. Then, I want you in bed with me," she added.

Nolan mentally repeated that *hell* and would have asked her if his bedmate status meant she wanted distraction sex, but the question died on his lips when he pulled into his driveway and spotted the dark green car parked in front of his house. Both Adalyn and he drew their guns, and he figured the agents in the SUV behind them did the same as the man who stepped from the car with his hands raised in the air.

Jeb.

Cursing, Nolan fired off a quick message for his

fellow agents to stand down, and he pulled up closer to the car to see Caroline hunkered down on the passenger seat. He certainly hadn't forgotten that he'd ordered Jeb to bring Caroline to him, but Nolan had expected the man to call to arrange a safe meeting place.

"Wait here," Nolan snarled to Jeb.

Nolan went ahead and pulled into the garage, and he quickly got Caroline inside. Once they'd cleared the place, he went back into the garage and motioned for Jeb to drive in. No way did he want Caroline exiting the vehicle while it was parked in front of his house. Of course, that meant bringing Jeb into the house as well, but Nolan couldn't allow his personal discomfort with the man to override the possibility of Caroline being killed.

It was obvious that Caroline had been doing a lot of crying. Her eyes were red, and she looked even more exhausted than Adalyn. Nolan motioned for her to go into the living room and sit on the sofa, and he went to the kitchen to get a pot of coffee started. While it was brewing, he brought out bottles of water for them. Adalyn got a fresh box of tissues for Caroline.

"Why would you risk bringing Caroline here?" Nolan snapped. "You should have had backup—"

"I did," Jeb interrupted. "I called my son and daughter, and they drove down. I trust them and both are lawmen. They might not always see eye to eye with me, but they're damn good at their jobs. They're parked just up the street."

Nolan went to the window and looked out. It wasn't

unusual for neighbors to have visitors park in front of their houses, and he soon spotted a black truck two houses away. The windows were heavily tinted so he couldn't see inside, but he had no doubts that Jeb's kids were there watching.

"They'll wait there, keeping an eye on the place, while we talk," Jeb explained. "Can you keep Caroline safe?" he came out and asked as he took the seat next to her.

Obviously, Jeb wasn't happy about being ordered to bring Caroline in. Tough. Nolan didn't care a rat about the man's annoyance.

"I'll keep her safe," Nolan assured him, and he prayed that was true. Prayed, too, that he'd get the right answers from the heap of questions he had for both Jeb and the woman. "Tell me about Russell Mason," Nolan started.

While Nolan opened a bottle of water, he took the chair across from Jeb and Caroline so he could study the man's reaction. At first, Jeb shook his head as if confused, but then Nolan saw the realization set in.

"Russell Mason," Jeb repeated. "Yeah, I remember somebody by that name. A big mess with his fiancée cheating on him and then shooting him. Why?" he tacked on to that without even pausing.

Nolan answered Jeb with another question of his own. "Do you recall that his fiancée resembled the Grave Digger's victims? Minus Caroline, of course." And to give his memory a boost, Nolan showed him a photo of Kimberly Charles.

"I remember her," Jeb immediately said, and now

the pause came. A pause he finished by muttering some mild profanity under his breath. "You think Russell's the Grave Digger?"

"Do you think he could be?" Nolan countered.

Blowing out a long breath, Jeb drank some water and eased his back against the sofa. "I just don't know. I haven't seen him in a long time, not for thirty years or more, but I can tell you he wasn't a happy camper when he left Lubbock County. He thought Kimberly should have gotten more jail time, and he blamed me for that."

Nolan didn't ask if Jeb blamed himself. Or if the blame was even justified. Cops didn't make deals to shave off jail time. That would have almost certainly come from the DA's office, and since Kimberly hadn't had a previous record, that would have played into her shortened sentence.

"Russell Mason's the man who kidnapped me?" Caroline asked, speaking for the first time since she'd been in the house.

"I'm considering he might be," Nolan said, and he left it at that.

He waited to see if either Jeb or Caroline was going to make the connection that Russell had lived in Lubbock County when Jeb's son had been taken, but neither of them jumped onto that particular train of thought. Since Nolan didn't especially want to go there, either, he moved on to the next subject.

"Before someone blew out the tires on my SUV, Adalyn and I had a chat with Donny Ray," Nolan said.

"He had a lot of things to say." Again, he waited, and this time he got a reaction.

From Caroline.

The woman's eyes widened, and she went pale. And that was the confirmation Nolan needed to know he sure as heck wasn't going to like the answers Caroline would give him. And one way or another, she would answer.

Caroline swallowed hard, and she turned to Jeb. "I'm going to ask you to do something hard. Something you're not going to want to do. But I need to talk to Nolan and Adalyn alone."

Jeb studied her with concerned eyes. "Why alone? What do you intend to tell them that I can't hear?"

"You will hear it," the woman insisted. "Just not right now. Right now, I need to get it all out, and that won't happen if you're in the room. Please, go ahead and call Leigh and Cash to let them know we're okay."

Jeb stood for some long moments, but he didn't immediately budge, and Nolan could see the debate the man was having with himself. He finally nodded.

"You can use my office," Nolan told him and pointed in the direction of the hall.

Caroline watched Jeb walk away, and then she slowly turned back to face Adalyn and him. "Donny Ray probably told you that I had a relationship with him." Her bottom lip trembled. "I was in love with him."

Nolan didn't confirm or deny what Donny Ray had said. He just waited for the woman to continue.

"I was working for Jeb at the time, but I didn't tell him about Donny Ray," she said. "I kept it secret because I knew Jeb wouldn't approve. Jeb was protective of me, and Donny Ray had a bad reputation."

Caroline paused, drank some water. "Donny Ray probably told you, too, that I've visited him in prison several times. Told Jeb I was going to see an old friend because I didn't want to explain what I was really doing." Her gaze met Nolan's. "Jeb really didn't like Donny Ray."

Then Jeb and he had something in common. Maybe even then, Jeb had seen the killer in the man.

"You're still in love with Donny Ray?" Adalyn asked, the sound of her voice cutting through the silence. The question surprised Nolan. It hadn't been on his radar to ask, but that was not surprise in Caroline's expression.

"No," the woman insisted, and then she seemed to break. "Maybe part of me still is. I don't want to be, but maybe I am." Tears spilled down her cheeks. She wiped them away, but more came. "I also don't want to believe the worst about him."

"He killed my father," Nolan said, trying and failing to keep the emotion out of his voice. "And he might be manipulating someone into killing for him. He might be behind the Grave Digger murders."

Caroline gasped and frantically shook her head. "No. Not the murders. Yes, I believe he killed your father, but that was an accident."

"He was gunning for me," Adalyn clarified. "So, Donny Ray went there with the intentions of murder. He just got the wrong person."

Caroline's breath broke in a hoarse sob. "I want

to believe his hot head got the worst of him, that he wouldn't have done that if he'd been thinking straight." She paused again. "I also don't want to believe he had a part in taking Jeb's son. But he might have. God, he might have."

Nolan moved to the edge of his chair, and Adalyn leaned over to pull out a handful of tissues for the woman. "What did Donny Ray do?" Nolan pressed.

"Maybe nothing," Caroline blurted out. "Maybe something horrible."

"Explain that," Nolan insisted.

Even though he'd snapped that out as an order, Caroline took several moments before she answered. "About six months ago, I got a text from an unknown number, and the person claimed to know who was responsible for Jeb's child being taken."

"Six months ago," Adalyn repeated, and Nolan knew why. That's when the Grave Digger's first victim had been discovered. "Did the texter tell you who they were, and did you save the phone?"

Caroline shook her head. "I got a phone with a different number and tossed the old one. And, no, he or she gave no name and just said that Jeb's son was taken by Donny Ray's former girlfriend who was jealous of me and wanted to get back at me. Maybe that's true. Donny Ray was seeing other women."

Yeah. He'd been seeing Gillian, and the timing might fit here. "Do you know the names of the other women?" Nolan asked.

Caroline shook her head again. "I didn't want to know. I want to believe he loved only me. I was stupid," she added in a mutter. "Because Donny Ray hated Jeb, too."

Nolan and Adalyn both stayed quiet. Waiting for Caroline to spell it all out for them. That the man she loved might not be just a killer and kidnapper, but that along with his "girlfriend," he might have orchestrated Caroline's own abduction.

"I have to tell Jeb all of this," Caroline said when she finally continued. "I need to ask for forgiveness."

"You need to do a lot more than that." Nolan took a breath. "I'm going to Mirandize you and get all of what you just told us on the record. It needs to be an official part of the investigation."

Frantically shaking her head, Caroline practically jumped to her feet. She looked ready to bolt, but they all turned in the direction of the footsteps.

Jeb.

He looked a little like a man in a trance when he came walking toward them, and he held up his phone. "Did you do this?" Jeb asked.

It took Nolan a moment to realize the question was directed at him. "Do what?"

"This," Jeb said, and he thrust the phone at Nolan.

Not at all sure of what he might see, Nolan took the phone and looked at the screen. "It's a report," he muttered. "For DNA results."

Results, comparing his own DNA to Jeb's.

Chapter Eleven

Because Adalyn had taken hold of Nolan's arms, she felt his muscles turn to iron. She turned him so she could see the phone screen for herself, and she could have sworn her heart skipped a couple of beats. Normally, Nolan was capable of doing that to her, but this had nothing to do with the intense attraction between them.

No.

It was because of what she read in the brief report. A report that claimed with 99.9 percent certainty that Jeb was Nolan's father.

"It's fake," Nolan said, his voice as hard as the muscles in his arm. "Where'd you get this? Who sent it to you?" He fired off those questions in rapid succession and aimed a glare at Jeb.

Jeb seemed the exact opposite of hard and glaring. He looked ready to collapse. "It came from an unknown sender," he managed to say.

Nolan cursed and whipped out his own phone. "I'm calling the lab because that's fake. It's just something else the Grave Digger is trying to use to muddy the waters."

Maybe, but Adalyn knew Nolan well enough to hear the doubts in his voice. He didn't put his phone on speaker, and he moved away from them as he made the call. Instead, he went to the window to look out. Adalyn joined him there and heard when he reached Steve Marquez, the lab tech whose name was on the report.

"This is Nolan Dalton," he snarled, and he rattled off his security access verification. "Confirm that you didn't process a DNA comparison on me."

"Special Agent Dalton," the tech said. His voice was a little shaky, maybe because of Nolan's fierce tone. "I did the comparison you requested and got back the results this afternoon. I just emailed them to you."

"I didn't request a comparison so who the hell did?" Nolan snapped.

"Uh, it's got your name on it, and it looks legit. It was just a standard paternity test to determine if Jeb Mercer was your biological father. He is."

There went her heart again. More beats lost, and she heard the thin rush of breath come from Nolan's mouth. Still, he regrouped quickly. "My DNA is on file, but where did you get the sample for the comparison?"

"Mercer's DNA was on file, too, since he's former law enforcement," the tech explained. "So, it was simple to see if there was a match."

The muscles tightened even more in Nolan's jaw. "It's a hoax. Someone put in the wrong DNA."

"Really? I don't see how. I got the DNA samples straight from the database, and just like you instructed, I also compared your DNA to Sheriffs Leigh and Cash Mercer. They matched as your siblings."

"I didn't instruct you to do anything with anyone in the Mercer family. Rerun the results now," Nolan ordered, and he stabbed End Call hard enough that she was surprised it didn't damage his phone.

"It's true," Jeb said, causing Nolan to whirl around and spear the man with his lethal gaze.

"Did you tamper with the database?" Nolan demanded.

Jeb shook his head. "No. And neither did Leigh or Cash."

"Then someone did. Russell could have done something like that," Nolan added in a mumble. "Hell, Cody, too. Or somebody working for Donny Ray could have been paid to hack in and change it." His gaze slashed to Caroline.

"I didn't have anything to do with this," Caroline insisted.

"Well, someone did," Nolan spit out like profanity.

"Maybe not," Jeb said. In contrast to Nolan's, his voice was calm and all reason. "Let me show you something. Something I did on my own. No tampering." With that same calmness, he walked closer, scrolled through to find something on his phone and he held it up for Nolan to see. Not a DNA report this time.

But two photos.

The side-by-side headshots were of toddler boys, both with dark brown hair and amber eyes. They weren't identical, but it was close enough for them to have been twins or brothers.

"The one on the left is my son," Jeb explained. "*Joe.* It was taken right before he went missing." He paused, cleared his throat. "The picture on the right is an age regression shot of you. No fakes, no tampering. I did the regression myself using your official photo from the FBI web page."

Oh, mercy.

That slammed into her hard, and Adalyn figured what she was feeling was a tiny drop in the bucket compared to Nolan's shock. Nolan didn't say anything. He just stood there, staring at the photos while he had a white-knuckle grip on his phone.

"Here's my theory," Jeb continued a moment later. His voice was still calm enough, but Adalyn could see that his hand was trembling. "Donny Ray or somebody pissed off at me took my boy." He turned to Caroline. "I heard what you told Adalyn and Nolan. Sorry. Thin walls, and uh, you weren't exactly whispering."

"Jeb," Caroline sobbed out. "I'm so sorry."

"We can get into that later," he assured her, and he slipped his arm around her waist. "For now, Nolan needs to hear this."

"Your *theory*," Nolan challenged.

Jeb nodded. "I believe Donny Ray or maybe somebody like Russell wanted to get back at me by taking my son. The person either sold him or gave him to someone."

Nolan took one menacing step toward Jeb. "You think my father bought me from a kidnapper?"

"No. I've researched Bill Dalton, and I believe he was a good man. I think whoever took Joe set it up as a private adoption and probably provided all the paperwork to make it look legal. Bill and your mom must have then decided not to tell you that you weren't their biological child."

Adalyn kept her mouth shut, but that theory sounded plausible to her. And if it was true, it would still cut Nolan to the core.

"It makes sense," Jeb went on when Nolan didn't respond. "The Grave Digger either found out you were my son or was the one behind your kidnapping, and that's why he dragged Caroline and me into this."

"Nothing about this makes sense," Nolan muttered while he continued to stare at the photos on Jeb's phone. He didn't resist when Adalyn slipped her arm around his waist and just held him.

"You really believe Donny Ray could have done all of this?" Caroline asked Jeb. The woman's voice cracked on her question. And Adalyn knew why the woman had fresh tears in her eyes. Because if Donny Ray was responsible, then it meant he'd maybe used her to get better access to Jeb. And to Jeb's son.

To Nolan.

Nolan might still be silently shaking his head over the possibility of his parentage, but Adalyn believed the DNA hadn't been faked. That the comparison had been done for one reason. To continue to take digs at Nolan. Maybe at Jeb, too. The Grave Digger would have known this shock would cloud their minds and maybe cause them to lose focus.

"I believe Donny Ray is capable of any and everything," Jeb answered. "And that's why we have to find the truth. We can maybe start with finding out how

Bill Dalton ended up with you. Where would he have kept adoption papers?" he added to Nolan.

Nolan didn't jump to answer, but after a few moments, he scrubbed his hand over his face. "In his office at the ranch. If the papers are there, they'd be in a filing cabinet next to his desk. I went through some of them after he died. But not all," he explained in a mutter.

Probably because going through them had been too painful.

"It's too risky to go to the ranch now," Nolan continued, "but I can send someone to search for them. Not Cody," he assured them. "Not until we're sure he's cleared."

Adalyn totally got the reason Nolan was having doubts about his fellow agent. It would have been a piece of cake for Cody to falsify the request for the DNA comparison. Then again, she could say the same for Russell. He certainly had the computer skills. Maybe Gillian and Jeremy did, too. And if they didn't have the skills, they could have hired someone.

When Jeb's phone dinged with a text, Nolan handed it back to the man. Bracing herself for the possibility this was another message from the Grave Digger, Adalyn pulled in her breath. Waiting. After seeing the stark look that came onto Jeb's face, she knew the bracing had been necessary.

"It's the Grave Digger?" Adalyn asked.

"No," Jeb said, heading toward the window. In the same motion, he drew his weapon. "The text is from my daughter. Leigh said someone's coming into the driveway. It's a man, and he has a gun."

NOLAN PUSHED ASIDE the gut punch of info he was trying to process and drew his gun. He hurried to the window, practically elbowing Jeb aside, and he looked outside. There was indeed a man exiting a car now parked in front of his house. A man wearing a shoulder holster.

Russell.

Judging from the way Russell was storming toward the house, he was a man on a mission, but Nolan didn't have time for this now. Not while he was still reeling from the news that he might be Jeb's son. And that was a strong *might*. The DNA could be faked, but there was no denying the photo comparison.

Later, he'd have to come to terms with that. Later, he'd have to come to terms with a lot of things, but for now he was apparently going to have to deal with Adalyn's former boss.

Russell hadn't even made it to the porch when Nolan spotted the trio of people get out of the black truck. A woman and two men.

"That's Leigh and Cash. The black-haired man is Leigh's fiancé, Cullen Brodie," Jeb verified.

That gave Nolan something else he had to push aside. He didn't look at Cash and Leigh to see if there was any family resemblance. Instead, Nolan pinned his attention to Russell and kept it there.

"Adalyn, get Caroline away from the windows," Nolan instructed.

Judging from the little huff Adalyn made, she'd rather be shoulder to shoulder with him, facing down Russell. But Nolan wanted both Caroline and her out of harm's way. Well, as much out of harm's way as he could manage, considering that one of their suspects stepped onto the porch.

The Mercer clan was right behind him. The woman, Leigh, was wearing jeans and her dark brown hair was scooped back into a ponytail. The man on her right shared enough of her features for Nolan to know it was Cash. Cullen was on her right.

"I'm Sheriff Leigh Mercer," the woman called out to Russell. "Put your hands in the air so I can see them and don't even think about going for your gun."

Russell stopped, spun around and found himself facing three drawn weapons. Actually, six, but he couldn't see the ones inside the house. Nolan didn't know Leigh, Cash or Cullen, but they looked formidable and fully capable of taking names and kicking some butt.

For now, Nolan welcomed their help. Because it was possible Russell hadn't come alone. Or this could be a ploy or distraction so the Grave Digger could get closer to the house so he could have another go at Caroline or Adalyn.

"I'm Russell Mason," he snapped. "Put down those guns."

"No," Cullen said, and it sounded both like a drawl and a very lethal snarl.

"But you'll put down yours." That came from Cash.

"Using just your fingers, lay that Glock on the porch and step to the side."

"Nolan, Adalyn," Russell snapped. "Get out here and tell these clowns who I am."

Nolan motioned for Jeb, Caroline and Adalyn to stay back while he disarmed the security system and opened the door. "Do as they said and put down your gun," Nolan warned Russell.

If looks could have killed, Russell would have ended Nolan on the spot. Still, Russell hesitated, as if debating the issue, but on some muttered profanity, he finally placed the Glock on the porch, and he stepped back from it. Only then did Cash and Leigh look at Nolan, and he knew that because he spared them a glance while Cullen kept his attention, and his SIG Sauer, homed in on Russell.

"I came here to help Adalyn and you," Russell snapped, and he put his hard glare on Nolan. "Where is she? I want to talk to her."

Nolan didn't want the man anywhere near Adalyn, but it wasn't safe to stand out in the open like this. A sniper might be willing to take on four guns if it meant getting to Adalyn or Caroline.

"Say what you have to say and leave," Nolan warned him. "Then, you can officially spell out what you say here in your interview tomorrow."

"I want to see Adalyn," Russell demanded, obviously ignoring what Nolan had just said.

"No." Nolan borrowed Cullen's firm but short response, and he stepped back as if to go inside.

"Wait," Russell practically shouted, and he mumbled something under his breath that Nolan didn't catch. "Just wait. And listen. Adalyn's at risk. So is Jeb Mercer, Caroline and anyone who happens to be around Adalyn when the Grave Digger comes for her."

"I'm listening," Nolan assured the man.

And he was keeping watch, too, though Leigh, Cash and Cullen were doing a darn good job of that. Cash had moved to the right side of the house. Cullen, to the left. Leigh was still dead center of the yard, and while she'd lowered her gun, she still had a two-handed grip on it, keeping it in a position where it'd be ready to fire.

"Make it fast," Nolan added when Russell didn't say anything. "You've got five minutes before I shut this door in your face."

"I found something else about Cody," Russell blurted out.

Nolan wanted to groan and ask why Russell had this sudden vendetta for Cody. But he had to consider that maybe it wasn't a vendetta at all but rather a possibility. One that Nolan hoped like the devil wasn't true.

"I found invoices for the purchases of cameras, timers and even the components for making explosives," Russell explained, "and they were paid for from a dummy account set up by Cody. I have copies of everything I found, and I can send them to you."

Now, Nolan did groan. "And how exactly did you come by that information?"

Russell glanced away. "I hacked into some files.

I know the info can't be used to make an arrest, but you can use it as a starting point. A way to find stuff that you can use to stop him."

Nolan stared at Russell. "Care to answer my question as to how you came by this?"

No glancing away this time. Russell hiked up his chin as if proud of his *accomplishment.* "I know how to dig for hidden accounts, and I found one under the name Cody Markham. That's his mother's maiden name."

"It could also be the name of dozens of other people," Nolan argued. But it was suspicious that the money had been used to pay for things the Grave Digger had used.

Well, maybe it had been.

It was possible Russell was making all of this up to try to cover up his own guilt. If so, it wasn't working. The man might truly be innocent, but there was nothing he could say that would make Nolan remove him from their list of suspects.

"There's more," Russell went on. "I think I know Cody's motives for the murders."

Nolan was already listening, but that got his attention. "What?" he demanded.

"I think he's got mommy issues. Bad ones."

Nolan thought back to the few times Cody had mentioned his parents. His dad had died when Cody was a baby, and his mother had raised him solo.

"I did some deep digging, and Elizabeth Markham Hill was not a good mother," Russell explained. "She was rich and mean as a snake. She purportedly treated him like dirt. He was in and out of the ER as a kid with bruises and broken bones that never got reported to the cops because of his mother's connections."

Childhood abuse could indeed create a wound that never healed. Worse, it could fester, and in extreme cases, it caused a person to kill. Nolan wasn't ready though to believe that was what had happened to Cody.

"There's something else," Russell continued. "According to the person I finally found who'd speak about Cody's mom, she used to duct tape his mouth and hands to punish him. Warped stuff," the man concluded. "My source didn't know about a connection to garbage bags, but there could be one."

"Does Cody's mother look like the Grave Digger's victims?" Nolan asked, knowing he'd check that for himself.

"The features are similar, yes, but it's more than that. With the exception of Caroline, the Grave Digger has gone after strong, independent women. So, I think he's killing both the looks and the type. Well, the type as he sees it anyway." Russell paused. "I think he's killing women who remind him of his abusive mother who was never punished for the things she did to him."

Nolan made a noncommittal sound, but again, it was something he'd press Cody about. First though, he wanted to get some answers from Russell.

"Done any DNA comparisons lately?" Nolan asked.

Russell looked surprised. And perhaps he was. But that wouldn't get him off the list, either. "What are you talking about?"

Nolan had no intention of spilling all, especially not in front of Leigh and Cash, so he chose his words carefully. "About someone making an illegal request through the crime lab. Do your hacking skills extend to doing something like that?"

Russell slowly shook his head while he studied Nolan. "No. What does this have to do with Cody and the Grave Digger?"

Maybe nothing.

Maybe everything.

But Nolan kept that to himself. "Your five minutes are more than up." He stepped back, and since he couldn't very well leave the others standing in his yard, he motioned for them to come inside.

"I need to talk to Adalyn," Russell insisted.

Nolan didn't respond, not with words anyway, but he kept his glare aimed at Russell until one by one, Leigh, Cash and Cullen were inside. Behind him, he heard the murmured "reunion" going on with Jeb, but Nolan ignored that, too. He waited until Russell dished out some raw profanity. Profanity all aimed at Nolan. And Nolan didn't go back inside until Russell had finally turned to leave.

Again, Nolan shut out what the others were saying, and he reset the security system before trying to call Cody. Adalyn came to him, keeping her gaze pinned to him. Probably looking for signs as to how this was affecting him. She knew him well enough to know this was eating away at him.

"Cody's still not answering," Nolan relayed to her when the call went to voice mail. "You heard what Russell said?"

She nodded. "You think the account actually belongs to Cody and he could be killing women to get back at his mother?"

He wished his answer could be a solid no, but Russell had managed to plant seeds of doubts. "I don't know," Nolan finally said. "I'll alert Marsha and have her demand Russell turn over any documents he found. Since what he did was a crime, I suspect his lawyer will try to shut it down. Marsha, in turn, can have forensic accountants start digging for any account under that name." An account that might or might not lead back to Cody.

Nolan took a moment to fire off a text to Marsha to tell her what was going on and request a thorough background check on Elizabeth Markham Hill. Then, he took another moment to slip his arm around Adalyn's waist and ease her to him. It wouldn't soothe the troubled look in her eyes. Wouldn't settle the knot in his gut, either. But he needed the close contact with her.

Across the room, Nolan could hear the murmured conversation Jeb was having with his kids, Cullen and Caroline, and Nolan didn't have to guess what they were talking about.

Him.

Jeb was almost certainly telling them about the

DNA match. That was Nolan's reminder to send another text, this time requesting an agent to go out to the ranch and retrieve documents from his father's files. It wouldn't be a quick process since the agent would first have to come by Nolan's place to get the keys for the ranch house.

Cash stepped away from the pack, and he met Nolan's gaze head-on. "I'm guessing you think the DNA results are…bogus?"

Nolan suspected Cash was about to use another word, one that wouldn't have been so polite. But at least Cash wasn't trying to insist that the results were the real deal. Not yet anyway.

"I'll be looking into it," Nolan assured him.

The corner of Cash's mouth lifted just a little in a very dry smile. "Yeah, so will I. Leigh will, too."

Nolan didn't have to be an FBI agent to pick up on the man's skepticism. "You think the results are… *bogus*?" Nolan asked.

Cash came closer. "I think I want proof so my family doesn't get twisted up again over a false claim. You see, we've had a lot of that over the years. Jeb's money is both a blessing and a curse. Let me see how I should put this." He made a show of tapping his chin as if thinking about it. "Jeb's stinking rich, and since Leigh and I both have opted out of any inheritance, our long-lost brother stands to gain a lot."

Nolan had to sift through everything Cash had just said. Through the doubt. Through the anger. At the core, Nolan thought there might be hope that the Mercers could finally have some peace over knowing the truth.

"Cash," Leigh said, joining them. Her voice was like a warning to her brother. "No need to get into all of this right now."

"I disagree," Cash argued. "How do we know Nolan didn't set up those DNA results?"

Now, Nolan got a dose of anger of his own. "I didn't. And even if it turns out that we do share the same gene pool, I don't want a dime of Jeb Mercer's money. In fact, I don't want anything from him or you."

That started a staring match between Cash and him. It also caused Leigh to groan and curse. Cullen stayed back, but Jeb came forward, no doubt ready to put in his two cents to this "family" discussion. However, Nolan got a pause button when his phone rang.

"That's probably Cody," he muttered to Adalyn, and he stepped back to take the call.

But it wasn't Cody's voice he heard when he answered. It was dispatch, who informed Nolan they were transferring a call to him.

From Gillian.

Nolan accepted the call, and Gillian immediately asked. "What have you done with him?"

It took Nolan a moment to regroup and shift gears. "What are you talking about?"

"Jeremy." Gillian's voice went up several notches in both volume and intensity. "He's not at his house or the office. He's missing."

Nolan was about to fire out some questions so he

could figure out what the hell was going on, but Gillian continued before he could say anything.

"Oh, God. There's blood. So much blood," Gillian said on a sob. "I think someone killed my brother."

Chapter Twelve

Adalyn kept herself busy, making sandwiches and coffee for the houseful of guests. She seriously doubted anyone was hungry, but it gave her something to do other than worry and pace. Of course, the worry was still there. And would be until they had some answers.

Now, there was a new question added to the mix of those answers they didn't have. Where was Jeremy? Had he actually been killed or kidnapped? Or was this all part of some scheme so he could disappear before the FBI could find proof that he was involved with the Grave Digger murders? Unfortunately, they wouldn't stand a chance of learning any of that until the man was found, alive, and could be questioned.

Nolan was in his office, coordinating the search for Jeremy. Along with doing a whole host of other things. That included talking to Cody, checking out the latest claims Russell had made, sifting through all the reports that were trickling in from the ERT. All of that while also dealing with the people under his roof who might or might not be his blood kin. Dealing, too, with his parents having kept secret that he'd been adopted.

Adalyn hadn't known Nolan's father that well, but she had to hope that he'd been a good man who wouldn't have engaged in something like an illegal adoption. Not knowingly anyway. But Nolan was going to have to brace himself for that possibility. If Bill and his wife had been desperate to have a child, they might have taken desperate measures. Measures where they ended up adopting and raising another family's stolen child.

"Need help?" Leigh asked, coming into the kitchen.

"Thanks, but I've got it." In fact, "got it" was an understatement because Adalyn lifted the tray with nearly a dozen sandwiches she'd made. "You can grab some chips though from the pantry."

Leigh nodded and went to do that, but she looked over her shoulder at Adalyn as she set the tray of sandwiches on the snack bar that divided the kitchen from the living room, where Cullen, Cash, Jeb and Caroline were seated.

"You used to be a cop?" Leigh said when she came back with two large bags of chips.

Adalyn nodded. "Jeb told you?"

"No. I saw it." Leigh motioned toward Adalyn's eyes. "That doesn't go away just because you no longer wear a badge. Just look at Jeb if you want proof."

Jeb. Not *Dad.* And while Adalyn tried to tamp down any reaction she had to that, obviously Leigh picked up on it, proving that she had cop's eyes of her own.

"Jeb and I aren't always on the same page. In fact, we're not exactly a close-knit family," Leigh added.

"Yet you came when he asked you to," Adalyn pointed out.

Leigh smiled a little. "Yeah, we did. Cop blood apparently overrides old family wounds."

Adalyn considered just changing the subject, but she wanted to know the dynamics going on so she could help Nolan deal. If it came down to dealing, that is. "Wounds caused in part by losing your brother?" Adalyn asked.

"In part," Leigh readily admitted. "Joe was the youngest. The kid brother. Daddy's little boy. Losing Joe sort of broke Jeb." She drew in a long, resigned breath. "And afterward, he didn't exactly have a lot of love to share with Cash and me. We sort of made our own way after that." She smiled again when she glanced at Cullen. "And we're both happy. Both engaged to be married. Both moving on. Jeb can't move on until he knows what happened to Joe."

"He believes Nolan is his son." Adalyn laid it all out there.

Leigh nodded. "I'm reserving judgment on that. And no, I don't buy that Nolan's doing this so he can dip into Jeb's very deep pockets. In fact, I think Nolan would prefer he not have a single cell of DNA in common with us Mercers."

She couldn't deny that. "Not because he has anything against you. It's because he loved his parents. From all accounts, they were a close-knit family, and he and his dad got even closer after his mom died."

Since that felt like too much personal info, Adalyn shifted gears. "Sandwiches are ready," she called out. "I'll take one into Nolan and check on him."

Adalyn put a sandwich and some chips on a plate, grabbed another bottle of water and went to Nolan's office. She found him doing exactly what she thought he would be doing. He was working on his computer while talking to someone on the phone. It only took her a few moments to realize he was finalizing the arrangements for a safe house.

He ended the call and looked up at her. "Thanks. And I'm sorry about leaving you alone with my *company*."

"It's okay," she assured him. "How are you?"

Nolan shrugged, but it wasn't a casual kind of response. Not with all the tension on his face. "The marshals will be here soon to move Caroline and Jeb to my father's ranch that they'll set up as a safe house."

"The ranch?" she asked, thinking of all the horrible memories that were there because it was where his father had died.

"I needed something fast," Nolan explained. "Something I could keep off FBI records in case there's a leak. Or in case Cody is, well, dirty. The ranch has a top-notch security system, and it's a big enough place in case the others want to go with Caroline and Jeb."

"I suspect they will." She opened the water he'd yet to touch and nudged the sandwich plate a little closer to him. He sighed, tore the sandwich in half and handed Adalyn a portion.

"Eat," Nolan insisted, "while I give you updates."

He took a small bite of his half of the ham and cheese and washed it down with some water before he continued. "No sign of Jeremy yet, but Gillian was right about the blood. There was plenty of it in Jeremy's house. Judging from the way things were tossed around, there was a struggle. A bad one that Jeremy didn't win."

Adalyn considered that while she picked up a chip, one that she hoped Nolan didn't notice that she wasn't eating. "You think the Grave Digger took him?"

"Possibly. Or Jeremy could have faked his attack and abduction. A lot of planning for that since he'd have to leave some of his own blood behind, but it's doable." Nolan paused, drank more water. "If the Grave Digger wanted him dead, why didn't he just kill him and leave the body?"

Yes, Adalyn had gone there as well. She'd also considered what the timing was for all of this. "Any guesses as to how long Jeremy had been missing before Gillian discovered the blood?"

"According to Gillian, she talked to him this morning around nine to make sure he'd be at the office to sign for an order that was expected at noon. She took the morning off to get some paperwork done at home and to pay us that visit at FBI headquarters. My guess is she didn't want her brother to know about that."

"No," Adalyn agreed, and she finally took a tiny bite of the chip when Nolan moved it closer to her mouth.

"Anyway, when the vendor called her to tell her Jeremy was a no-show, she went looking for him,"

Nolan continued. "So, there's a bout a five-hour time frame where he could have been taken or set things up to look as if he'd been abducted."

Five hours. That meant they couldn't rule out Russell or Gillian. The woman could have decided to off her own brother if Jeremy had found out she was making it possible for Donny Ray to play out the part of the Grave Digger. If so, it was a "nice" touch to have worked in a visit to FBI headquarters to present a front of being a cooperative person of interest.

"We don't have anything yet on that account Russell told me about," Nolan went on, "but I do have the background on Cody's mother." He paused a moment. "She was as bad as Russell claimed she was. I tried to contact her, but I got her assistant who passed on a message that she wouldn't discuss her worthless son with anyone."

"Wow," Adalyn remarked. "Any indications that Cody did something to make him seem worthless in her eyes?"

"Nothing on the surface, but there were multiple visits for Cody to the ER, just as Russell said."

She shook her head. "Wouldn't some of this have come up in Cody's background check when he applied to the FBI Academy?"

"It would have, but Cody could have insisted it hadn't left him with any mental scars."

Yes, and he'd obviously been convincing enough because he'd indeed passed the check. And that could mean, well, nothing. Maybe the childhood abuse wasn't a factor here.

"One more thing," Nolan went on. "The adoption papers were in my dad's old files. They were taken into evidence and will be examined for, well, anything that could connect to what's happening now."

"Uh, are you okay with that?" she wanted to know.

He knew she wasn't just asking about the papers themselves but rather the history behind them. His kidnapping, being sold to his parents. The fact that he was Joe Mercer.

"I'm working on being okay with it," he assured her. She figured that was going to be a long process for him to come to terms with everything.

"What can I do to help?" Adalyn asked a moment later. Nolan looked at her. Studying her. "Yes, I know. I look worn-out and exhausted. Added to that, some of my bruises are now a nasty color combination of purple and green."

He smiled, took hold of her hand and eased her down. Onto his lap. "And yet you still manage to look amazing."

Adalyn gave him a fake smile, but oh, that drawl and his eyes had done the job of nudging aside some of the fatigue and making her remember why Nolan and she had become lovers in the first place. It was because of this hot energy that seemed to zing between them whenever they were together.

Like now.

Since that heat was rising with every passing second, it didn't surprise her when Nolan slipped his hand around the back of her neck, drew her in and put his mouth on hers. She got another zing of that energy, of that intense attraction, and this one kiss was more than enough to cause the heat to slide through her entire body.

She had missed this. The instant surrender of her body to him. The aching need that notched up when he deepened the kiss. His taste was all Nolan. Something branded into her. Something that would be the benchmark for any and all other kisses. So far, no one else had lived up to what Nolan could give her. What he could make her feel.

Adalyn shifted so she could put her arms around him and draw him closer. Of course, that created some interesting contact since her butt was now on his lap. All that touching. All that heat.

And the need skyrocketed.

The kiss didn't stay gentle. Couldn't. Because they were suddenly starved for each other, and it didn't take long before they started grappling for position. Trying to get closer. Trying to make the fire burn hotter and hotter while soothing all the hurt and pain.

"We shouldn't be doing this," he managed to say.

Truer words had never been spoken. They had a houseful of people and a killer to catch. Nolan's to-do list was a mile long. Still, he didn't stop. He kept kissing and moved his hand to the front of her shirt.

When he flicked his thumb over her nipple—which wasn't hard to find since it was puckered against her bra—Adalyn knew she couldn't take much more of this without dragging him to the floor. Something she was strongly considering.

When Nolan's phone rang.

Cursing, he fumbled to pick it up from his desk while Adalyn somehow maneuvered off his lap. No easy feat. Not with her body still burning for Nolan. Still, they couldn't just skip calls to make out or have sex. And that was proof positive of the distraction this kind of heat could cause.

"It's the prison," Nolan relayed to her.

That got her attention because it could be Cody with an update. If so, then Nolan could ask him about the bank account Russell claimed to have found. But it wasn't Cody. It was Donny Ray's voice that oozed through the room.

"I guess you didn't get what you wanted from me so you sent up your lackey to talk to me," Donny Ray greeted.

"If you mean Agent Cody Hill, he's not a lackey," Nolan fired right back, and he pushed the record function on his phone. "Is he still there with you?"

"No, he left hours ago, but after he was gone, I got to thinking that I should probably be clearing up a few things. Things that might put my butt in a sling with the appeal. Plus, I hear confession's good for the soul and all of that."

"You've got something you want to confess?" Nolan asked.

"Sure do. Buckle up, Nolan, because you're not gonna like much of what I'm about to say."

"I'm listening," he assured him when Donny Ray didn't jump to add anything else.

Adalyn was listening, too. Along with holding her breath. She didn't want to get up her hopes that Donny

Ray could or would help them. Still, he might give them something, all to avoid his butt in a sling. She reminded herself though that this could be just another taunt. One of Donny Ray's ploys to take a poke at old wounds.

"Jeremy came to visit me a while back," Donny Ray finally continued. "I had my lawyer bring him in so the conversation wouldn't be recorded because there were things I didn't want others overhearing."

"Illegal things," Nolan provided. "Did you ask Jeremy to kill for you, to set up the persona of the Grave Digger?"

"No." Donny Ray sounded surprised, and Adalyn wished she could see the man's face so she stood a chance of knowing if that surprise was the real deal. "Is that what he told you?" he snapped.

"Is that what you did?" Nolan countered.

"No, hell no. I didn't tell him to kill anybody." Donny Ray paused. "But he might have decided to do that all on his own."

Adalyn felt the pressure build in her chest. Was Donny Ray going to hand them Jeremy?

"Why would Jeremy decide to kill someone?" Nolan asked. He was all FBI agent now and was keeping the emotion out of it.

Donny Ray cursed, then groaned. "Look, I'm already on death row so don't even bother trying to prosecute me for it."

"Prosecute you for what?" Nolan snapped.

There was more groaning, more cursing. "For stealing Jeb Mercer's kid."

Adalyn certainly hadn't expected that to come out of Donny Ray's mouth. Apparently, neither had Nolan because his breath went a little thin. Again, she suspected there was a much bigger reaction than that below the surface.

"I did it to get back at Jeb," Donny Ray went on. "Because he'd messed me over, and I wanted to mess with him."

"You messed with him all right." Nolan's voice was tight, like a coil ready to break. "Did Caroline help you?"

"No. I wouldn't have trusted her. She was all about loyalty to Jeb even back then. No," Donny Ray repeated. "I took the kid on my own with the lure of going to the barn to see some puppies. I took *you*."

Those last three words seemed to suck every drop of air out of the room. Adalyn wasn't even sure she could manage to speak. But Nolan did.

"How do you know it was me?" he asked.

"Because I'm the one who took you to Bill and Mary Dalton."

Those words hit just as hard as the others, and this time, Nolan took a moment, no doubt to try to rein in all the emotions that had to be slamming into him. "How did you know them?" Nolan pressed.

"I had a cousin who was thinking about being a surrogate. Bill and Mary's surrogate," Donny Ray qualified. "She told me they were going to pay her ten grand plus all her medical expenses but that she was having second thoughts about doing it. Wasn't sure she could give up the kid once it was born."

Nolan had a long drink of water before he said, "So, you offered them me?"

"Yeah. I made up a story about you being my girlfriend's kid and that she was having some trouble and was going to have to put you in foster care. I had some papers drawn up. Ones that must have looked official enough since they paid me and took you."

Now, Nolan cursed. "You want me to believe that two law-abiding people didn't question a child being brought to their doorstep?"

"Oh, they questioned it, but in the end they bought it because they wanted a kid. They wanted a kid more than just about anything so they took you and paid me the money they'd planned on giving a surrogate."

"Why the hell should I believe one word of this?" Nolan snarled.

"Because it's true. And because in a roundabout way, it leads back to Jeremy. I told him all of this six months ago. Told him I was worried about it all coming back to bite me. You know, because if you and Adalyn found out, you might dig in harder and make it impossible for me to win an appeal."

Nolan huffed. "You think Jeremy is killing for you?"

"Maybe. Jeremy can have a hot head, and he still uses drugs. Gillian doesn't know," Donny Ray quickly added but then paused. "Or at least she pretends she doesn't. She loves him and might not want to see the truth."

"I could turn that around and say the same about Gillian. Maybe she's the one killing for you. Maybe she's the Grave Digger."

"No, no, no. You're dead wrong about that. Gillian loves me, and I love her."

"People in love do stupid things," Nolan fired back, "and this entire conversation could be to get some of the heat off her. I'm looking at her, you know. Looking for any- and everything I can use to arrest her for murdering for you."

"No." And this time, Donny Ray shouted it. "You gotta listen to me."

"Then, tell me the truth." Nolan spoke through clenched teeth.

Donny Ray paused for a long time. "All right, the truth. I was going to confess to all of this during the appeal, but there's no reason for you not to hear it now. That night, the night I shot Bill, that was all an accident. I didn't go there with the intention of killing anybody."

Because she needed something to steady her, Adalyn clamped her hand on Nolan's shoulder. "You went there gunning for me," she managed to say.

"No," Donny Ray said on a heavy sigh. He didn't seem the least bit surprised that she'd been listening to this conversation. "Let me back up a little. A couple days before that night, Bill paid me a visit. Don't know how the hell he found me, but he did, and he said his conscience was bothering him. That he wanted to come clean with Nolan about being adopted."

Adalyn already knew the answer, but she looked down at Nolan to see if he'd known about any of this. He shook his head. And she hoped he remembered the source, that this might not even be true.

But it felt true.

Heaven help them, it felt very true.

"Bill said he thought the paperwork I gave him was bogus," Donny Ray went on, "and he demanded to know the names of your birth parents. I didn't tell him, of course. Couldn't. He would have gone straight to Jeb, and he would have figured out a way to arrest me."

The muscles stirred in Nolan's jaw. "He had a right to arrest you."

"Oh, Jeb wouldn't have ended with just an arrest. With his connections, he would have figured out a way to bury me. That's why I went to see Bill that night. I had to talk him out of pushing to clear his conscience. But when I saw Adalyn there, I figured he was about to tell her everything. I snapped. And I fired."

Adalyn shook her head, trying to force her mind to grasp what she'd just heard. "You weren't trying to kill me?" she asked.

"No," Donny Ray answered. "Even though it was all done in hot blood, which my lawyer says was temporary insanity, I hit my target that night. I shot Nolan's dad."

Chapter Thirteen

Nolan wasn't sure he could speak or move. It turned out though that he didn't have to do either because Donny Ray ended the call. Maybe to gloat over the firestorm he'd caused inside Nolan. Maybe to laugh over taking another jab at Adalyn and him.

But this didn't feel like a jab.

He wanted to dismiss it all, to shove it aside and never think about it again. About his parents buying him. About him being stolen from Jeb Mercer.

About his father being Donny Ray's target.

All these months he'd believed Adalyn was the reason for that fatal shot, but Nolan knew that Donny Ray had been telling the truth.

Nolan groaned, and he pressed his fists on the sides of his temples. He had to hand it to Adalyn. She didn't try to hold him or soothe him. She simply got up, went to the small bar area in his office and poured him a generous shot of his favorite whiskey.

"Drink this," she insisted.

He did. Nolan downed it and welcomed the burn

that went from his throat to his gut. It was better than feeling the ball of ice that'd settled there.

Adalyn sat on the edge of the desk, took his face in her hands. "I'm sorry."

"I'm sorry," he echoed back. And it was also the truth.

Nolan regretted all the bad feelings he'd had when he'd believed his father was dead all because of Donny Ray gunning for her. They'd ended their relationship not because of those bad feelings, but because he hadn't been able to get past his grief. Well, he sure as hell had to get past it now because all of this could be the reason the Grave Digger was killing.

"I need to find Jeremy," he said, hoping by speaking it aloud that it would help line up his thoughts. He had to line them up. Had to think. Because his grief and pain could end up getting someone killed.

"You can talk about it if you want," Adalyn offered.

He shook his head. He didn't want to talk. Or remember. At the moment, he had no memories whatsoever of Lubbock County. Of being Jeb Mercer's son. No memories of a young Donny Ray luring him away.

And Nolan wanted to keep it that way, at least a little longer.

"All right then." Adalyn brushed her mouth against his.

Nolan might have taken more from her. He might have deepened that kiss so the heat would take away more of the cold. But his phone rang.

Yanking himself out of his thoughts, he saw Cody's

name on the screen. He tried to make the shift from the messed-up kidnapped son to the FBI agent that he was. The work and the investigation would keep him grounded, and right now, he very much needed that.

Along with needing answers from Cody.

Nolan hoped Cody had an alibi for the time Jeremy had gone missing. Or at least a good explanation as for why he'd been out of touch.

"Cody," Nolan answered, and he put the call on speaker. "Where are you?"

"On my way back from the prison." There was no defensiveness in his voice. It seemed a normal agent-to-fellow-agent tone. "I'm heading home to change before I go into work. I heard about Jeremy, and I'll see if I can get any leads on that. I also need to write up my report on Donny Ray."

"Did you get the visitors logs?" Nolan asked.

"They should be in our inbox within the next hour or so. But there was a problem with the recorded conversations. The files were corrupted somehow. Yeah," Cody added when Nolan cursed. "I'm thinking Donny Ray might have bribed somebody to do the corrupting, and I want to take a hard look at Russell Mason."

"Russell," Nolan repeated. "He paid Adalyn and me a visit, and he claims he hacked into a bank account that belongs to you. An account under the name Cody Markham."

Cody rattled off a string of profanity. "I don't have an account under any name but my own. That SOB is trying to frame me because I'm getting close to arresting him."

Nolan couldn't discount that, but there was the other matter. "Russell told me about your mother, and I ran a check on her."

Cody cursed again. "Oh, let me guess. Russell said because I have a lousy mom, that it's turned me into a killer. It hasn't," he insisted.

"But she was a lousy mom," Nolan said, testing the waters.

"Damn right, she was. She smacked me around when I was a kid and told me I'd never amount to anything. Well, she was wrong." His voice had gotten louder with each word, and he practically shouted out the last sentence. "I am somebody," Cody added in a hoarse whisper.

Nolan wanted to keep pushing, but he decided it was best to wait until he was face to face with Cody for that.

"When Russell was tossing around nonexistent dirt on me, did he also mention that his name is on the visitors log, that he came to see Donny Ray about six months ago? Six months," Cody emphasized.

Nolan knew the significance of the timing. It was when the Grave Digger had started killing.

"Did Donny Ray happen to say why Russell had visited him?" Nolan pressed.

"I didn't get a chance to ask him. I'd already finished my conversation with him when I got my first look at the logs. By then, Donny Ray was in a meeting with his lawyer and wouldn't see me. I figured once I was back at the office, I'd try to call Donny

Ray and then arrange for Russell to be brought in for an interview."

"He's already scheduled for one first thing in the morning," Nolan informed him.

"Good, because I want him in the box. I'm not going to let him get away with trying to smear my name."

The level of anger seemed right enough. *Seemed.* But Nolan didn't want to trust his instincts on this. Not when so much was at stake.

"You think Russell could be working for Donny Ray, that he could be the Grave Digger?" Nolan came out and asked.

"It's possible," Cody answered. "If Russell hasn't gone off the deep end and is killing his cheating fiancée, then maybe he has a different reason for the murders. I read in your report that Russell and Donny Ray lived in Lubbock County around the same time. They could have been friends. Close friends, and now Russell could be killing for his old friend."

Unfortunately, Nolan didn't need Cody or anyone else to fill in the blanks for him on this. Donny Ray could have orchestrated the Grave Digger murders so the finger wouldn't point to him when and if Caroline was taken. And murdered. The Grave Digger would get the blame, not Donny Ray.

"Why would Russell go along with something like that?" Nolan asked.

"Maybe because Donny Ray's paying him lots and lots of money. Or it could be that Donny Ray was just his inspiration for getting started. Either way, I want to talk to both men and see what they have to say."

"So do I," Nolan assured him. "You'll also want to clear up Russell's allegations about the bank account. It's best to go ahead and get your statement on the record."

Now, Cody wasn't so quick to answer, and he cursed again. "Okay, you're right," Cody finally agreed. "I'm pulling into my driveway right now. As soon as I'm at the office, I'll get started—"

Nolan had no trouble hearing the loud blast that came from the other end of the phone. Not an explosion. But he certainly recognized the sound.

Gunfire.

Cody made a sharp groan of pain. "Nolan, I need help. I've been shot."

Hell. That was not what Nolan had wanted to hear.

"How bad are you hurt?" Nolan asked, already getting up from his desk and heading to his office door.

Cody didn't answer, but there was another blast of gunfire.

"I'm calling for an ambulance and backup," Nolan added, hoping that Cody could hear him. Hoping that Cody was alive. "I'll be at your place in a couple of minutes."

With Adalyn hurrying along right behind him, Nolan had to hang up on Cody, and he made those calls while he grabbed his keys. That obviously got the attention of his houseguests, and they gathered closer to him, no doubt waiting to hear what was going on.

"My partner was shot," Nolan blurted out. He scribbled down the code for the security system and took out his backup remote device from one of the drawers. "Use this to reset the system when I'm gone."

"Wait," Adalyn insisted, and she took hold of his arm. "You can't go alone. This could be a trap to lure you out. A trap to try to get to Caroline," she added.

"Cody could be bleeding out," he reminded her. The adrenaline was pushing him to move now, but Nolan stopped, and he forced himself to think this through.

Because Adalyn was right.

Backup was already on the way to Cody's and would likely be there even before he could make it. The ambulance would have to stay back if there was still active gunfire, but it would be in place once the scene was secure. Cody would get the medical attention he needed. But right now, Adalyn and the others needed attention, too. This might not be just a trap to lure him out and get to Caroline but to also get to Adalyn.

"All right," Nolan said, and he mentally worked through some possible scenarios as to how this could play out. There weren't a lot of good options here.

"I'll go with you," Adalyn suggested. "You'll need backup on the drive over to Cody's."

Yeah, he probably would, but Nolan hated that it would possibly come from her.

Adalyn moved closer, made eye contact with him. "If Caroline and I are the targets, we shouldn't be here together," she whispered. "We force the killer's hand. Either come after me when I'm with you or try to break into the house and take Caroline."

Adalyn had no doubt kept her voice low so she wouldn't alarm Caroline with that, but the woman obviously heard, and she gasped. Jeb put his arm around her, but he kept his attention on Nolan.

"My suggestion," Jeb said, "Leigh and Cullen can go with Adalyn and you. Cash and I can stay here with Caroline."

Nolan debated the logistics of that, and it was a little unbalanced since it could basically leave Cash to defend Caroline if the killer attacked the house. Jeb had plenty of cop experience, but he wasn't in his prime.

"Cash and I can go with Nolan," Adalyn suggested, letting Nolan know that they were on the same page. "Leigh and Cullen can stay here with you. That way, you can keep watch on all sides of the house to make sure no one is trying to sneak up and jam the security system."

Nolan didn't give anyone a chance to discuss or debate that plan. He'd already lost precious minutes so with a hitch of his thumb for Cash and Adalyn to follow him, he paused the security system long enough for them to get into the garage.

"You take the back seat," Nolan instructed Adalyn. "Cash will ride shotgun." And he hoped like the devil that Cash was as good of a lawman as he appeared to be. It was possible when they got to Cody's, they might be caught up in gunfire.

Once Nolan was in the loaner SUV he was still using, he tried to call Cody again. It was a risk since a gunman could maybe use the sound of the phone to home in on Cody if he was pinned down. But Nolan also needed a status report. He needed to know if Cody was alive.

"The call went to voice mail," Nolan relayed to Adalyn and Cash.

Nolan didn't drive away from the house until the garage door was shut. He also didn't have to tell Adalyn and Cash to keep watch because they both were already doing that. Along with both of them also having their weapons drawn and ready.

It was only a five-minute drive to Cody's, but it wouldn't be a fast one since he'd have to travel through neighborhoods where there'd maybe be kids playing and slower moving traffic. It'd eat up too much valuable time for him to circle around to the highway.

Without taking his eyes off the road and their surroundings, Nolan passed his phone back to Adalyn. "Call Marsha and try to get an update on backup and the ambulance."

Adalyn made a sound of agreement, and Nolan had no doubts that she'd be able to get whatever info was available. That's why he focused on looking for a killer or any signs of attack.

And there was one.

One second, Nolan was slowing for a stop sign just ahead, and the next, the jolt felt as if they'd slammed into a truck.

The blast ripped through the SUV.

No, not through it but from *beneath* it. Maybe from an explosive device that'd been set on the road. He cursed himself for not realizing that the killer would have known he'd have to take this route. It could turn out to be a fatal mistake.

Again, the airbags deployed, and Nolan felt the now-familiar snap of the seat belt clamp around him. Vising him. Pinning him in. Just as it'd done the day before when they'd been coming back from the prison.

Nolan managed to glance in the rearview mirror, and he saw Adalyn. Alive. But there was already shock on her face, and her shooting hand was hampered because of the side airbags.

Cursing, Cash slapped away the airbag, trying to get ready in case they were attacked.

That came, too.

The bullet crashed into the window, right where Adalyn was sitting. His heart jumped to his throat, but he didn't see any blood. She hadn't been hit. The bullet resistant glass had held. For now anyway. But the gunman was obviously trying to do something about that because another shot slammed into the window.

"Get down!" Nolan yelled to her, and Adalyn managed to untangle herself from the seat belt and airbag so she could lower herself to the floor.

Nolan whipped around in his seat to try to pinpoint the location of the shooter. Cash did the same, but Nolan knew the man was seeing what he was. Plenty of possible hiding places from the houses that lined both sides of the street. Added to that, there were lots of huge live oak trees with dense-enough branches where a sniper could conceal himself.

He tried to start the SUV with the hopes he could

drive them out of there. But the engine was clearly too damaged. Which had almost certainly been the killer's goal all along. He wanted them here like sitting ducks, waiting to be picked off. The SOB didn't care that innocent bystanders could be hurt or killed in the process.

Another shot came, right in the same spot as the others, and this time, the glass gave way and exploded through the interior of the SUV. It rained down on Adalyn so Nolan leaned in and tried to cover her head.

He heard his phone ring and realized that Adalyn still had hold of it, but he shut out the sound and focused on the shooter. Beside him, Cash was doing the same.

"There," Cash said, pointing to a side yard between two houses.

Nolan caught a glimpse of someone wearing bulky clothes and a ski mask. The person had a rifle aimed at them and fired off two more shots. Both blasted through the now-glassless window and exited on the other side.

And then the shooter turned and took off running.

Hell. He was getting away.

Nolan's first instinct was to throw open the door and go after him. Obviously, it was Cash's instinct, too, but they stopped and looked at each other. They didn't exactly have an entire unspoken conversation, but something came through loud and clear. If they went out there, a second shooter could be in place to gun them down.

And take or kill Adalyn.

That couldn't happen. It was especially troubling because now that the shots had stopped, some people were coming out from cover. The Grave Digger or his hired gun wouldn't hesitate to kill every last one of them.

"I need my phone," Nolan told Adalyn, and while he reached down to get it from her, he did another quick check to make sure she was okay. She was clearly shaken, but she was holding it together.

His phone rang again before he could call for help, and Marsha's name appeared on the screen. Good. This would save him a step.

"Someone tried to blow up the SUV I'm using, and then fired shots at us," Nolan told her the second he answered. He rattled off the street address. "Get somebody out here ASAP."

"Will do," Marsha assured him, and he heard her relay his orders to someone, probably a fellow agent. "Are Adalyn or you hurt?"

"No." Maybe that was true. "What about Cody?"

"Ambulance and backup are at his house. All I know right now is that he was shot but is alive. I don't know if his injuries are serious."

"Stay on that," Nolan instructed. "I need an update."

The scream stopped him from adding anything else, and Nolan fired glances around to see a woman running from the area where he'd last spotted the shooter.

"He's been shot!" she yelled. "He needs help."

Nolan cursed again and had another debate with himself. "Wait here with Adalyn," he finally told Cash. "Marsha, I need another ambulance out here."

He added a "Stay down" reminder to Adalyn, and he got out and ran toward the screaming, hysterical woman.

He got just a glimpse of the SUV and realized he'd been right about the explosive being set on the road. Other than the bullet-shattered windows, the damage was mainly to the front end. To the engine. The killer had wanted to make sure they didn't just drive out of there.

Keeping watch around him, Nolan hurried past the woman, who was now being comforted by another neighbor, and he had no trouble seeing the man lying on the ground. A man wearing bulky clothes and a ski mask. But Nolan was pretty sure this guy wouldn't be needing any help.

Because he was already dead.

ADALYN WENT THROUGH the bits and pieces of info she'd learned over the past hour since she'd gotten back to Nolan's house. Cody was alive and was at the hospital being treated for his injuries.

That was the good news.

The bad was that his shooter had vanished before backup had arrived so the FBI didn't know who was responsible for the attack. It was the same for the latest one on Cash, Nolan and her. The dead man found near the scene was being transported to the medical examiner so he could be IDed. Maybe then, they'd have answers, but Adalyn suspected the shooters had been hired guns. Hired by the Grave Digger, who was likely one of their suspects.

Gillian, Jeremy or Russell.

Cody was off the list because of the shooting so that was at least one thing cleared up. Plus, it put the spotlight on Russell since he'd been so adamant about Cody being a dirty agent. Adalyn was sure the FBI would be questioning Russell about that. Questioning Gillian, too. And Jeremy once they located the man.

The sound of the footsteps and murmured good-byes pulled Adalyn out of her thoughts. With Leigh and Cullen right behind her, she stood just inside the door that led to Nolan's garage and watched as the two marshals ushered Caroline, Cash and Jeb into a large SUV so they could be taken to the ranch.

There was another identical SUV beside it, and both had been parked inside the now-closed garage so everyone could load up. Since the windows were heavily tinted, it would hopefully be hard for anyone watching to figure out which vehicle had the passengers.

That was just one of the precautions that Nolan had arranged. The marshals would keep watch to try to spot anyone following them, and Jeb, Cash and Caroline had also turned over their cell phones and been given burners so the devices couldn't be used to trace their location.

Leigh and Cullen waved goodbye to Caroline and their family members, and then they turned to Adalyn to repeat the farewell to her. Cash had been able to arrange his schedule so he could go to the safe house with Jeb, but Leigh and Cullen had to get back to Lubbock County.

"You'll make sure Nolan's okay?" Leigh asked her and surprised Adalyn by pulling her into a hug.

"I will," Adalyn assured her. Though she knew Nolan was far from okay. She could hear him snarling out orders to whoever was on the receiving end of his latest phone call.

As Nolan had instructed him to do, Cullen shut the garage door after the marshals were gone, and the three of them went back into the kitchen to see Nolan while he was on the phone. His expression was fierce, all warrior now. A warrior who was no doubt blaming himself for this latest attack.

Nolan had said a quick goodbye to Jeb, Cash and Caroline, and now he gave Cullen and Leigh a brusque wave, but on a sigh, Leigh went into the kitchen and hugged him. Nolan froze for just a second, but he returned the hug and told the caller to "Hold on a second."

"Keep me updated," Leigh said to him in a whisper. "Keep them safe."

"I'll do my best. It might not be good enough though."

Leigh sighed again, nodded. "It'll be good enough."

Nolan didn't look at all convinced of that, but he continued his phone conversation as Adalyn went to the front door with Leigh and Cullen. Once they were outside and in their truck, Adalyn waved goodbye, and again following Nolan's instructions, she locked the door and immediately reset the security system.

While she waited for Nolan to finish his call, Adalyn started a fresh pot of coffee. Since she already felt wired, she probably didn't need the caffeine, but she figured they had a long night ahead of them. No way would Nolan take any downtime with all the things he was juggling.

The coffee had just finished brewing by the time Nolan ended his latest call, and he muttered a thanks when she poured him a cup. He blew at it, took a sip and then closed his eyes a moment.

"Jeremy's dead," he said.

Adalyn's hand froze when she reached for her own cup of coffee. "They found his body?"

"They did at the scene of the shooting. He wasn't far from the other dead guy we saw."

Needing a moment, Adalyn just leaned against the kitchen counter. "Jeremy was one of the gunmen?"

Nolan shrugged. "He had the rifle so it's possible he's the one who shot at Cody, but the ME thinks the angle of the gunshot wound to Jeremy's chest is off for a self-inflicted injury."

Adalyn needed yet another moment to process that. "He was maybe kidnapped and then set up?"

"It's looking that way," Nolan agreed.

So, they were back to Gillian and Russell, but Adalyn had to wonder if Gillian could have done that to her own brother. Then again, family members sometimes killed each other. She'd seen that when she'd been a cop.

"What about Cody?" she asked.

Nolan's jaw tightened a little. "Flesh wound. He's already been discharged from the hospital and is back at home."

She heard the doubts in Nolan's voice. Doubts that Cody might indeed have been behind all of the attacks. And maybe was even the Grave Digger. That possibility was only adding the guilt that was already eating away at Nolan.

"I nearly got you killed today," he said.

She'd been right about the guilt.

Adalyn did something about that. She took his coffee, setting it on the counter, and grabbed a fistful of the front of his shirt. She hauled him to her and kissed him. It wouldn't help with the investigation, probably wouldn't help with the guilt, either, but for a couple of seconds she wanted him to feel something other than this bone-weary misery. She wanted that for herself, too.

And she got it.

The heat from the kiss both soothed and aroused. A reminder that Nolan had a way of accomplishing both. So, she gave him a reminder as well. Of just how much need there was simmering between them. Kissing wouldn't fix anything, but it seemed as necessary and vital as the air she was breathing.

She eased back, looked up at him. The heat was in his eyes now, and some of the fatigue was gone. Both good signs. So, Adalyn kissed him again. She halfway expected for him to put a quick stop to this, but he didn't. In fact, he was the one who deepened the kiss.

A sound of raw need grumbled in his throat, and he snapped her to him. In the same motion, he turned her so that the small of her back was against the counter. Then, he went in for another kiss. Then, another.

"You know my phone is going to ring and interrupt us," he grumbled.

Probably. It'd been ringing practically nonstop since the last attack, and since they couldn't ignore any calls, it would certainly be an interruption. For now though, they just kissed as if there was nothing wrong in their world.

Nolan's arm tightened around her waist while he moved his other hand between them. She expected him to touch. To move this make-out session to second base, but he went many steps beyond that by taking hold of her top and pulling it off over her head. He didn't stop there. Nolan lowered his very hot, very clever mouth, and he shoved down the cups of her bra and gave her some kisses she knew she'd never forget.

Adalyn didn't have to ask where this intense heat had come from. It'd been there for days, simmering, and now they'd obviously reached the boiling-over stage.

Since they'd both obviously given in to the moment, she went after his shoulder holster and shirt as well. He was bruised, battered. And incredible. Even now, she could appreciate that rangy, muscled body. A warrior's body to go along with that expression he was still sporting. It took her straight into overdrive.

Nolan was apparently on the same overdrive page as she was because he went after her jeans. Adalyn helped with that. Helped fuel the fierce that battle that was suddenly going on between them.

He shimmied off her jeans and slide holster and then lowered her to the floor. Good. Even though there were beds only yards away, her body was telling her it had to be now. It had to be Nolan.

Always Nolan.

Adalyn hadn't needed this to know how much she cared for him. Or how much she still loved him. But it was a solid reminder.

While he kept kissing and touching her, while he drove her mad with need, she tackled his jeans. Not easy since he was pressing hard against the zipper. Still, she got him unzipped and was ready to push both his jeans and boxers off his hips when he caught onto her hand to stop her. She groaned and for a moment thought she'd missed the sound of his phone ringing. It would have been easy to do since her pulse was pounding in her ears.

"Condom," Nolan gutted out.

Oh. That. She'd completely forgotten the whole safe sex angle to this. That's because the need had turned to a relentless ache that would not be denied.

Nolan thankfully didn't deny her. He took a condom from his wallet, and while he was getting it on, she managed to lower his jeans and boxers enough. Then, Adalyn pulled him on top of her.

Despite the hard floor against her back, it was like coming home, Christmas and her birthday all rolled into one. Definitely memorable, just like the man himself.

Nolan cupped her head, turning her to make eye contact, while he pushed inside her. His eyes heated even more, and he made a husky groan of pleasure.

Adalyn did her own groaning, and she had no doubts that the heat was mirrored in her own eyes.

This level of heat wouldn't last for her. She'd been this route with him before, and he knew how to push her right to the edge. Fast and hard. There'd be more once he'd taken off the edge for her. More, more, more until they'd sated each other. That wouldn't last, either. Because she knew she'd need him all over again.

For now though, Adalyn just allowed him to take her up, up, up to that peak. Nolan touched her, moved inside her and made it impossible for her to do anything else.

But surrender.

Chapter Fourteen

Nolan had no intention of dwelling on the mistake he'd made by having sex with Adalyn. Dwelling sure as hell wouldn't do any good right now, and besides, the sex had cleared his mind.

Sort of.

His mind was now skirting around the fact that he'd managed to get Adalyn in his bed for their second round. A round that had obviously exhausted her because she was now asleep in his arms. And naked. His body wasn't going to let him forget that detail, and it stirred a fresh heat inside him. Still, Adalyn, the heat and his relaxed muscles made it easier to focus on other things.

Bad things.

But he couldn't just shove that away and pretend all was well with the world. It wasn't. The Grave Digger was still out there, one of their suspects was dead, another injured, and Nolan still didn't know if Donny Ray was behind the Grave Digger attacks or if someone like Cody or Russell was doing all of this on their own. Unfortunately, it wasn't something he might learn unless there was another attack. Definitely not a thought that would help him sleep better tonight.

At least Jeb, Caroline and Cash were tucked in at the ranch. That was a plus, and even though the marshals hadn't stayed at the ranch with them, Jeb and Cash had agreed to take turns standing watch, and they'd turned on the security system. Since every door and window in the place was set with an alarm, an intruder wouldn't get in without them knowing about it. And that's why Nolan was considering if he should take Adalyn there as well.

It'd be uncomfortable being under the same roof with the man who believed he was his father.

Nolan stopped. Rethought that and silently cursed.

Because Jeb Mercer likely was his father. Hell, he could even take out the *likely*. Jeb was his father. Everything pointed to that, and once the killer had been identified and put away, then Nolan would need to deal with that. Deal with the fact, too, that the man who'd raised him had lied to him and had made a deal with the devil to get a son. A deal that'd come back to haunt him when Donny Ray had gunned him down.

Yeah, there were a lot of things he was going to have to face.

For now though, he settled himself against Adalyn and tried to get some sleep. That lasted about ten seconds before his phone rang. Adalyn practically jackknifed to a sitting position, and even though she had to be exhausted, she went from sound asleep to full alert.

"It's Cody," he told her after he glanced at the screen.

He took a deep breath that he figured he'd need and put the call on speaker.

"They still haven't found the guy who shot me," Cody said right off. "But I heard they IDed Jeremy as the shooter."

"Jeremy was in the vicinity," Nolan corrected. "I'm not sure he was the gunman."

Cody went silent for several moments, and Nolan couldn't help but wonder if he was silently cursing because he'd wanted all of this pinned on Jeremy. "Then, we might have two missing shooters," Cody concluded.

"Sounds that way. One could have been the Grave Digger or both could have been hired guns. I put in a request to have the forensic accountants to dig for any secret account Donny Ray might be using to pay for lackeys." That was one of the many calls Nolan had made today.

"Good. That's good. Because he could be tapping into funds from the woman he killed."

That was Nolan's theory, too, if Donny Ray was actually behind the murders and attacks. Right now, that was still a big if.

"Are you and Adalyn okay?" Cody asked a moment later.

"Shaken up but fine," Nolan settled for saying. "How about you?"

"Shaken up but fine," Cody repeated. "Get some rest, Nolan, and we'll start hunting for a killer tomorrow."

Nolan made a sound of agreement and ended the call, but his phone rang before he could even put it back on the nightstand. It was Marsha this time, and he figured his conversation with her wouldn't put a knot in his gut the way it had with Cody.

"Give me good news," Nolan said when he answered.

"Uh, I lost two pounds on my new diet," Marsha replied. "Unfortunately, that's about it in the good-news department. Russell delayed the interview again. Said he had a doctor's appointment. He's now scheduled to arrive four hours later than originally planned."

Great. The man was stalling. "What about the photos from the camera he had installed outside Adalyn's house?"

"We got those, and the lab guys say there's a man in the shots all right. It was someone from the city checking Adalyn's water meter."

So, not Cody as Russell had claimed. "You verified the city sent someone out?"

"Sure did. So, either Russell jumped the gun on his claim or else he wanted to stir up trouble. Let me know if you figure out which."

Nolan would definitely do that. "What about Gillian? Any sign of her?"

"Last I heard she was making funeral arrangements for her brother. I did the notification of death myself, and she seemed shaken up."

"Seemed?" Nolan repeated. "Any vibe that she was faking it?"

"I'm an FBI agent, which means I'm cynical to the bone. I think nearly every person of interest is faking it." She paused, sighed. "But, no, there were no waving red flags announcing that she'd offed her own brother."

Nolan totally got that cynical-to-the-bone part. He was feeling that way about all their persons of interest.

"I'll link you into the interview with Russell," Marsha went on. "Figured you wouldn't want to bring Adalyn to headquarters after what happened today."

"No," Nolan quietly agreed.

"Hope that's the last of the explosives. Requisitions can't be happy with all these SUVs getting blown up. Try to keep the latest one intact," she added before she signed off.

That was a reminder that the "latest one," another black SUV, was now parked in his garage. He'd had to move out when the marshals had come to pick up Jeb, Caroline and Cash, but after Adalyn's and his rounds of sex, Nolan had pulled it into the garage. After he'd scanned it for explosives.

Yeah, he wanted to keep this one intact.

Even more, he wanted to keep Adalyn safe.

He turned to the woman he intended to keep safe and saw that she was staring at him. A déjà vu moment since he'd seen that look from her before. While she'd been naked in his bed. It was a warm invitation for him to kiss her. So, that's what he did.

Nolan eased her to him and sank right into the kiss. He shoved aside all doubts about this complicating the heck out of an already complicated situation. He just took and Adalyn gave.

The heat was instant, and he would have kept on

taking if the sound of his ringing phone hadn't stopped him. Cursing, he looked at the screen and saw the number of the burner cell that the marshals had given Jeb.

Nolan's stomach dropped.

"Is something wrong?" Nolan asked the moment he answered.

"Yeah," Jeb verified. "Caroline saw Russell near the house, and she ran outside after him. She's holding him at gunpoint and won't back down. She says she's going to kill him because he's the one who kidnapped her and put her in that grave."

ADALYN GOT OUT of the bed, fast, and started dressing. She hoped that Nolan wasn't planning on giving her any grief about going to the ranch with him, but he was in the hurry mode, too. No way did he want to arrange for someone to babysit her when they might finally have the Grave Digger.

Might.

That one word was like a neon sign in her mind, and she knew they'd have to be careful in case this was a ruse to draw them out for another attack, but the *might* lost ground when Adalyn asked herself one question.

What was Russell doing at the ranch?

She was guessing he hadn't had good intentions when he'd shown up there, and she was thankful that Caroline had spotted him. What Adalyn wasn't thankful for was the woman running out of the house to put that gun on him. Obviously, Nolan was worried about that, too, because he practically threw on his clothes and made the call for backup while they hurried into the garage.

"Keep watch," he told her, and he took off, turning on the blue flashing lights on the dash. "We'll get there before backup, but I'm taking a different route than I normally would. Just in case the killer's planted more explosives on the road."

That didn't help tamp down the adrenaline that was already flooding through her, and Adalyn figured Nolan was feeling plenty of it, too. This could be it. The break they'd been looking for. They might finally be able to put away a killer. The danger could end. But first, they had to get there in one piece.

While he sped through roads that threaded out of the city and into the countryside, Nolan used the hands-free to call Jeb. Thankfully, the man answered on the first ring.

"I'm about fifteen minutes out," Nolan told him. "What's your status?"

"Caroline still won't come inside, and she won't give me the gun. I don't want to push it because I think she's right on the edge. I'm hoping she'll listen to you when you get here."

Adalyn was hoping the same thing. They didn't want Russell dead because then he wouldn't be able to give them answers. There could be other victims. Other explosives. And Adalyn wanted to hear him say why he'd done all of this.

If he had in fact done all of this, that is.

She couldn't focus solely on him until she was certain he was indeed the Grave Digger.

"Tell me why Caroline ended up going outside and how she managed to get her hands on a gun," Nolan insisted.

The breath Jeb took was heavy and long. "She apparently saw Russell out the kitchen window, and she grabbed one of the backup weapons Cash had brought with him. She must have gotten the jump on him because by the time I got outside, she'd already fired a shot at Russell and had gotten him to toss down his own gun."

Adalyn groaned. Caroline was lucky that Russell hadn't been the one to get the jump on her.

"Caroline believes he's the one who kidnapped her and that he came here tonight to kill her," Jeb added.

"And what does Russell have to say about that?" Nolan pressed. It was the very question Adalyn had been about to ask.

"Nothing," Jeb spit out. "He's clammed up, but at least at the moment he's not trying to get away. That might have something to do with Cash and me also having guns trained on him. Still, I'd rather Caroline not be outside like this. When you get here, we need to get her back inside."

"Agreed," Nolan said. "Russell could have brought a hired gun or two with him. Remind Caroline of that and see if it helps to get her moving."

"I'll try, but I've never seen her like this. I think the trauma from nearly dying has hit her full force.

Her hands are shaking, and she keeps telling Russell she's going to make him pay."

Adalyn could hear the woman vowing to do just that. Since Caroline was so adamant that Russell had been the one to kidnap her, maybe she'd remembered something. Something that could be used to verify that he had indeed been the one who'd taken her and put her in the ground. Even though this seemed like a slam dunk by catching Russell so close to the house, the FBI would still need to build a case to arrest him for murder. Right now, the best they'd be able to get him for was trespassing.

"Keep talking to Caroline," Nolan instructed. "Keep trying to convince her to go inside."

"Will do," Jeb assured him, and they ended the call.

Nolan kept driving, kept speeding through the back roads. Thankfully, there wasn't any traffic to speak of, and he had some decent visibility because of a nearly full moon. This was ranch and farming land with the houses positioned acres apart. Far better position than the attack that'd gone on in Nolan's neighborhood. Still, there was the disadvantage of backup. The ranch definitely wasn't on the beaten path.

Since she wasn't that familiar with this route, Adalyn didn't recognize anything until she spotted the large white house just ahead. The house where Nolan's father had been murdered. Just seeing it gave her a bad jolt of memories, but she tried to push all that aside. Tried to keep her focus on what was happening now.

After Nolan turned into the driveway, it didn't take

long for her to spot Caroline and the others. Russell was on his knees, his hands tucked behind his head, while Cash, Caroline and Jeb had weapons trained on him. Since Russell's head was down, Adalyn couldn't see his expression, and she wished she could. Maybe she'd be able to tell if it was true, that he was the Grave Digger.

Caroline didn't take her gaze off Russell even when Nolan pulled to a stop just yards away from her. He turned off the blue lights but kept the headlights on to better illuminate the yard. They definitely needed that. The moon was covered by clouds, and the lights coming from inside the house weren't nearly enough for them to spot anyone hiding behind the apparent forest of trees that were on the grounds.

With their guns already drawn, Nolan and she stepped out of the SUV together.

"Caroline, go inside the house with Adalyn and Jeb," Nolan ordered, sounding very much like the FBI agent that he was.

Now, the woman glanced at him, and Adalyn knew why Jeb hadn't pushed to get that gun away from her. Caroline's eyes were wild, and she was indeed shaking. One push the wrong way, and she'd no doubt pull that trigger.

"I'm not going to let him try to kill me," Caroline said on a hoarse sob.

"He won't get the chance to do that," Nolan assured her, walking past Jeb to get closer to the woman. "Because I'm going to arrest him. Now, go inside with Jeb and Adalyn. It's not safe for Jeb to be out here."

Caroline blinked in surprise, and some of the wildness eased in her eyes. "I don't want Jeb hurt, but I don't want the Grave Digger to get away."

"He won't," Nolan assured her.

He went even closer and slowly closed his left hand over the gun she was holding. Nolan didn't jerk it away from her. He inched it out of her grip, and the moment he had it, Jeb moved in to take hold of Caroline. The woman dropped her head on his shoulder and started sobbing.

"Go with them," Nolan told Adalyn, and he gave her a brief glance, maybe to see if she'd argue about that.

She wouldn't. The faster she got Caroline inside, the better. "Bring Russell in, too," she insisted, though she didn't exactly relish the idea of being under the same roof with him. Still, it would get Nolan and Cash inside as well. "Backup is still a good twenty minutes out."

Nolan nodded, and that was her cue to get Jeb and Caroline moving. Cash held his position with his gun still trained on Russell while Nolan took a pair of plastic restraints from his pocket.

Thankfully, Jeb hurried things along by scooping Caroline up in his arms, and they hurried to the back porch. Adalyn didn't let down her guard because she had no idea just how carefully Cash and Jeb had been watching the back of the house when they'd been guarding Russell. She didn't want to run into one of the Grave Digger's henchmen who'd managed to sneak in.

They went into the kitchen. Familiar ground for her since she'd chatted with Nolan's dad here while he'd been cooking dinner on that fatal night.

"Wait here and watch Caroline and the door," Jeb said, easing Caroline onto one of the chairs at the kitchen table. "I'll check the house."

Adalyn didn't turn down that offer. Someone needed to make sure no one else was inside, and this way she'd still be able to keep an eye on Russell, Nolan and Cash. She did that, all the while volleying glances at Caroline and the rest of the yard.

"I couldn't let him take me again," Caroline muttered. She was still crying, still shaking, but Adalyn stayed on watch.

"No one is going to take you." And Adalyn prayed that was true. She definitely didn't have a good feeling about this.

The tension in her chest eased a bit when she saw Nolan and Cash start leading the now-cuffed Russell toward the house. He continued to keep his head down, and since his mouth wasn't moving, he was staying silent.

Jeb still hadn't returned from the house search when Nolan finally stepped in with Russell. "On the floor," Nolan ordered the man, and he positioned him facedown just on the other side of the counter that divided the kitchen from the massive living room.

"He had this in his ear," Nolan said, holding up a small transmitter for Adalyn to see.

Her stomach dropped because it meant Russell

likely wasn't working alone. "Who's helping you?" she snapped, figuring the question was useless.

It was. Because Nolan didn't answer.

Adalyn heard the footsteps on the stairs, and Cash, Nolan and she all pivoted in that direction. She caught just a glimpse of Jeb.

He wasn't alone.

Adalyn jerked in her breath, took aim and got another glimpse of the person wearing a ski mask behind him.

Just as the lights went out.

NOLAN FELT THE fresh punch of adrenaline roar through his entire body. The fresh punch of fear, too. Not fear for himself but for Jeb, Adalyn and Caroline. He hadn't managed to see the person behind Jeb, but Nolan couldn't miss the gun he or she had aimed at Jeb's head.

"Get down," Nolan managed to say, and he hoped both Adalyn and Caroline would do just that.

He also took cover and thought he heard Cash do that same. Good thing, too, because the sound of the gunshot blasted through the house.

Hell.

Had the intruder shot Jeb?

Maybe—Nolan just couldn't see, and his eyes weren't making a fast adjustment to the sudden darkness. However, there was nothing wrong with his hearing, and there was plenty of movement that was seemingly coming from all directions at once. He believed one of those sounds was a moan of pain from Jeb.

"Jeb!" Caroline shouted, and judging from the grunts and sounds of a struggle, the woman was trying to get to him.

Nolan didn't want her to do that because the other sounds he heard let him know that Jeb might be in a fight for his life. Along with the moans of pain, there was also the sound of fists flying.

"It's me," Cash said, moving past Nolan and toward the spot where they'd last seen Jeb.

He wanted to tell Cash to stay back, but Nolan wouldn't have if their positions had been reversed. Besides, the man was already hurrying. His boots landing against the hardwood floor echoed through the house and sounded like muffled gunfire. But Nolan was almost certain that not all of those footsteps belonged to Cash. Either the intruder had managed to break away from Jeb...

Or someone else was in the house.

Nolan pivoted when he heard the slight squeak of the back door opening, and his eyes had adjusted enough to see the shadowy figure there who was dressed all in black. He barely had time for that to register when the person lifted a gun and fired a shot. Nolan dived to the floor so he could try to maneuver in front of Adalyn and Caroline.

Another shot came at him, and that's when he saw the person was wearing some kind of goggles. Maybe night vision. If so, he or she had a huge advantage. But there was something else on the person's face, too. A gas mask.

Caroline screamed, her voice blending with the

other sounds, and Nolan tried to get to her, but more shots stopped him. So did the thud of something that'd dropped on the kitchen floor. Not a footstep or a boot this time.

A tear gas canister that immediately started to spew out the chemicals.

It acted fast. It was only a few seconds before Nolan's eyes started to water, and he began to cough. He wasn't alone in that, either. Everyone not wearing a gas mask would be affected. Including Russell. He heard the man curse as the coughing fit overtook him.

Nolan had no control over the violent coughing that was tearing at his lungs and throat, and he sure as hell couldn't see, but he still tried to get to Adalyn. Nolan was pretty sure some of those coughs belonged to her so he tried to use them to home in on her position. That's when he heard somebody moving around.

Toward the back door.

Where the shooter was likely still standing. Waiting to gun them all down.

Still, it would be instinct to try to get to fresh air, and that was no doubt what Adalyn and Caroline were doing. Nolan went in that direction and hoped he could tackle the shooter before he got off another shot.

It seemed to take an eternity for him to get the few yards to the door, and he gulped in some air before he realized no one was there. The shooter was gone. But that wasn't exactly a comforting thought because he or she could be anywhere.

Behind him, he heard the struggle still going on with Jeb, Cash and whoever it was they were battling. Nolan hoped they could handle what was happening because he crawled onto the porch, looking for Caroline and Adalyn. His eyes were burning like crazy, making it hard to focus, but he didn't see them. Didn't hear them.

"Adalyn?" he risked saying, knowing full well that the shooter could use the sound of his voice to pinpoint his location.

But no shots came.

Inside, the lights flared on, and the sound of movement stopped. Just stopped. Nolan thought his heart might have as well since he fired glances around him and didn't see Adalyn.

Jumping to his feet, he frantically looked around the yard. Not there. So, he hurried back in the house. The kitchen was empty, but there were some smears of blood on the floor.

The coughing started again, and his eyes watered, but Nolan could still see that Russell wasn't there, either. His first thought, a gut-punching horrible one, was that the man had managed to escape and had taken Caroline and Adalyn with him.

"It's me," he heard Cash say again.

Cash was coughing hard, but he had his left arm hooked around Jeb's waist and was leading him to the back door. Nolan couldn't see any gunshot wounds, but he caught a glimpse of the lifeless body by the stairs.

Nolan helped Cash get Jeb onto the porch, and once he'd gathered his breath, he bolted into the yard. "I need to find Adalyn and Caroline," he managed to say.

That got Cash's attention. "They're not in the house?"

"Not unless they managed to get upstairs."

Nolan would check there next if he didn't find them in the yard. He held on to the hope they'd gotten away from the house and were hiding in case there was another attack.

Then, his phone dinged with a text.

Even though it was a risk to take his eyes off his surroundings, he did just that when he checked and saw Unknown on the screen. But Nolan knew exactly who this was.

The Grave Digger.

A thousand thoughts went through his head, none good, and he forced himself to read the message.

Let's play a game. I have Adalyn and Caroline, the text said. I'll give you a chance to save them. A small chance anyway. Stay tuned for more info, Nolan, and brace yourself. It's going to be a fun night.

Chapter Fifteen

Adalyn knew she was dreaming. Caught up in a nightmare. One where the Grave Digger had her and was putting her in the ground. As usual, she fought. She tried to get away. But her arms and legs wouldn't move.

She heard herself moan and was thankful for it. Because it meant she was coming out of the dream. It meant she could steady her breathing and understand that she was safe.

But she wasn't.

She wasn't safe at all.

That realization caused her to open her eyes. Or at least that's what she tried to do, but it was dark. So dark. She couldn't see anything, and her head was spinning.

"A blindfold," she murmured to herself before she could panic.

She wasn't blind. There was just something over her eyes. Something tied around her hands, too.

"Nolan?" Adalyn said, knowing he wasn't there. If he had been, she wouldn't be bound. Mercy, did that mean he'd been hurt? Or worse.

Was he dead?

Since she couldn't bear the thought of that, she pushed it aside and told herself that he was alive. He had to be alive. She couldn't lose him. And he felt the same way about her. One way or another, he'd get to her, and she had to just hold on to that.

Around her, she heard someone moving. Heard more moans, too, but these weren't coming from her. *Caroline*. That thought flashed through her head. Maybe Caroline or Nolan was here with her after all.

Wherever *here* was.

Adalyn pressed her lips together. She wasn't gagged, but her mouth was numb and felt as watery and limp as the rest of her. Even through the whirling in her head, she knew she'd been drugged.

"Who's there?" she managed to ask. She had to clear her throat and repeat it, just so it'd have some sound.

There was more movement, and someone yanked off her blindfold. Someone wearing a hazmat suit that concealed his or her face and body. And that's when she knew.

The Grave Digger had her.

She rolled to the side so she could run. Or rather that's what she tried to do, but her body didn't respond. Whatever drug she'd been given, it was doing its job, making it hard for her to fight back. But not impossible. She had no intention of just lying there and giving up.

Adalyn glanced around to get her bearings. She was in the woods, surrounded by trees and underbrush. She was still dressed, but the right sleeve of her shirt was missing. And she wasn't alone. Caroline was only a few feet away, blindfolded and gagged, and her hands were bound with the Grave Digger's favorite tool.

Duct tape.

The woman whimpered, her head whipping from side to side, and she was no doubt reliving the nightmare she'd already experienced once before.

Nolan wasn't there. Neither were Cash or Jeb, and she remembered the gunshots she'd heard when they'd been at the house. Maybe they'd been hurt. But maybe they'd managed to do the hurting and had taken out the henchmen who'd been sent in after them.

"Who are you?" Adalyn asked the person in the hazmat suit. She tried, and failed, to make that seem like an order.

The person laughed. Not a human sound. No. It was more like a cartoon character, which meant he or she was using a voice distorter. Unfortunately, they weren't hard to come by, and it made it impossible to tell who she was dealing with. Maybe Cody or Gillian. Heck, maybe even Russell since she wasn't sure if he'd managed to escape once the tear gas had gone off in the house.

"We're going to have some fun," the monster said in that sickeningly happy voice.

What little breath she had stalled in her throat when Adalyn turned her head to the side and saw the two shallow graves, and she caught the scent of the freshly dug dirt. Again, she had to fight off the panic. It wouldn't help, and she couldn't give in to it.

"Caroline first," the killer said. "Since she dodged death last time, she gets first go tonight. Of course, I had to modify my signature some. Less duct tape. But this will still get the job done."

Behind the gag, Caroline began to mutter more of those frantic sounds, and she struggled. It didn't do her any good though. The killer dragged her to the grave that was just deep and wide enough for her to fit inside.

"I do love it when they fight," the killer taunted.

"Good," Adalyn said, hoping to draw his or her attention off Caroline. "Because you'll get a fight from me, you worthless SOB. Why deal with Caroline when she's not going to give you much fun?"

"Oh, because she's the one who got away. Can't have that, can we?"

The teasing question was just what she needed. Adalyn felt the anger rise in her throat. Felt the kick of energy from the adrenaline. She wasn't sure if she had enough strength to get up, but she tried anyway and managed to lift her head and shoulders off the ground.

The killer scrambled to her. And got right in her face. So close that she could hear the rapid, excited breaths.

She stared into the hazmat visor, hoping to see the face on the other side, but the snake had put in a mirrored surface so all she saw was her own reflection. At least there wasn't terror in her eyes even if she was feeling an ample amount of that. No. She thankfully looked ready to rip this monster limb from limb.

The killer laughed again, and Adalyn twisted her body around and managed to deliver a kick to the side. No laughter now. Some cartoon cursing, and the killer latched on to her hair, yanking back her head so hard that the pain shot through her.

"You want to see what I sent to your boyfriend?" the Grave Digger asked, holding up a phone. "Want to see what already has him running to find you?"

Now, more terror came, but Adalyn forced herself to look at the message that was already on the screen. It was directions. No doubt ones that would lead Nolan from the ranch to here.

Where the Grave Digger would try to kill him.

"Text him back and lie. Tell him to go to another location to find me," Adalyn said. "You've got me. I'm your victim, not Nolan."

"Oh, that's so touching. Must be true love."

It was, but she had no intention of baring her soul about being in love with the man she was now trying to save. "It's a big risk to bring Nolan here. He'll kill you."

Another laugh. "He'll try, but he'll be so focused on trying to dig you out of the ground that he won't see it coming. Bye-bye, Nolan."

It wasn't hatred she heard in the voice. Something else below the distorted tones. Obsession, maybe. Or maybe these were just the words and actions of a sociopath hell-bent on killing.

Adalyn choked back a sob when the Grave Digger did send another text to Nolan. "Hurry, lover boy. She's nearly dead."

"How long before he's here?" Adalyn asked, not certain at all that she'd get an answer.

"Not long at all. In fact, I expect to hear the pitter-patter of cowboy boots here in the next ten minutes or so. That's why I need to finish."

Still in a squatting position, the killer turned to start covering Caroline with the mound of dirt that was beside the grave. Adalyn figured it was now or never.

Using her bound hands, she punched the killer in the ribs, and even through the hazmat suit, she must have caused some pain because he or she cursed and whirled back around. Adalyn used that motion, adding some of her own. She kicked out, taking the killer's feet right out from underneath him.

She didn't wait to see where he or she had landed, Adalyn rolled away, and despite her wobbly legs, she got into a crouch. Hardly the best fighting position, but it was better than being on her back.

"Run, Caroline," she called out to the woman.

Thankfully, Caroline didn't just lie there and moan. She sat up, and digging her elbows into the ground, she tried to get out of the grave.

The killer went after her.

Adalyn did something about that, too. With her head still spinning, she stood, lowered her head and ran toward her target. She rammed into his back with as much force as she could muster. Which wasn't much. But it was still enough to throw him off balance. The killer fell, sprawling out on the ground.

For once, Adalyn was thankful for the hazmat suit. It was bulky and made maneuvering hard. Just hard enough for her to hurry to Caroline. Adalyn couldn't grab on to her because her own hands were still bound, but she pushed Caroline in the direction of a cluster of trees.

"We have to run," she whispered to Caroline. "It's our only chance."

What Adalyn wouldn't admit was that the chance was slim to none. Still, she had no intention of making it easy for the Grave Digger to make her nightmare come to life.

Adalyn got the woman moving again while she tried to listen for the killer. She didn't hear him, but she heard something else. Something that turned everything inside her icy cold.

"Adalyn?" she heard Nolan call out.

The killer's cartoon laugh echoed through the woods for just a split second before the blast of gunfire drowned it out.

WHEN NOLAN SAW the person in the hazmat suit take aim at him, he ducked behind one of the massive live oaks in the woods a split second before the bullet hit the tree and sent out a spray of splinters.

Across from him, Jeb and Cash took cover as well and readied their guns in case they got a safe chance to return fire. They hadn't waited for backup. The moment Nolan had gotten the text, he'd started running to get to his SUV, and Jeb and Cash had followed him.

A text with directions that led to the very back of the ranch.

Thankfully, there'd been a trail leading to the location where he'd taken Caroline and Adalyn. It was the same trail the killer had obviously used because Nolan had found the black van.

Empty.

He hadn't taken the time to search for any proof of ownership but had instead followed the map so he could try to save Adalyn and Caroline. He would get to them in time. There was no other option. He wasn't going to lose either of them to a killer that he intended to put down tonight.

"Your henchman's dead back at the house," Nolan called out.

It got the reaction he expected. Another shot came his way, and he heard the distorted cursing that followed. "You're too early."

That loosened some of the muscles from the vise they had on Nolan's chest. Too early meant they were still alive. Well, hopefully, it did.

Across from him, he saw Cash motion toward a section of the woods to Nolan's right. He didn't have a clear line of sight of that area, but when Nolan leaned out from the tree, he saw Adalyn.

Yes, she was alive, thank God.

Caroline was crouched behind her, and they'd hunkered down. That was another plus, but that didn't mean they were out of danger. No, if the Grave Digger started firing in their direction, they'd still be easy targets.

And that's why Nolan had to do something about that.

He leaned out the left side of the tree, and since he

knew it was a safe shot to take, he fired at the killer. He'd probably missed, but that was because he didn't know the SOB's exact location. He or she had taken cover, too, and could be behind any of the trees on the other side of the small clearing where two graves sat.

Nolan tried not to think about those graves, about how the killer had no doubt delighted in telling Adalyn that it was where she would die. The Grave Digger would pay for that. Nolan would see to it.

"Too much of a coward to come out and face me?" Nolan taunted. He wanted to keep the killer's focus, and shots, on him.

Again, Nolan got an expected response. A third shot. This one went a little wide, slamming into the tree behind Nolan. Maybe the aim was just off or it could mean the killer was moving.

Trying to get to Adalyn and Caroline.

Nolan glanced in the women's direction again, and this time he saw Adalyn using her teeth to try to chew off the duct tape that had been wound around her wrists. He couldn't take the chance that she'd be able to get out of those in time so Nolan fired another shot to get the killer's attention.

He didn't get it.

Nolan cursed when there was no return of gunfire, no sound whatsoever.

"Get to Adalyn and Caroline," Nolan whispered to Cash. "I'll go this way and try to get behind him. Or her," he added because he knew very well that it could be Gillian in that suit.

Staying low, Cash and Jeb started toward the

women, and Nolan didn't waste even a second doing what he had to do. And what he wanted to do was kill the killer before anyone else was harmed or murdered.

Nolan threaded his way through the trees and underbrush. Listening and trying to pick through the darkness and the shadows. All the while he hoped Cash and Jeb were doing the same.

He tried to steady the heartbeat crashing in his ears, and he paused a moment to try to hear any movement. None. Hell. Had the killer just run off because they'd spoiled his plans by arriving a little early? An early arrival that'd happened only because Nolan had driven like a bat out of hell to get to Adalyn.

Maybe the snake was gone.

But Nolan figured he was doing what snakes like him did, lying in wait.

It was a risk, but he clamped his penlight between his teeth and turned it on, aiming it at the ground. And that's when he saw it. Not the killer.

It was the hazmat suit.

So, he or she had shed their disguise. Or maybe it'd been more than that. After all, the ERTs who'd processed the Grave Digger's crime scenes hadn't found a single shred of useful evidence. Maybe because the hazmat suit had prevented anything from being left behind.

He kept moving, kept looking. And it wasn't long before he spotted something else. Something he recognized. It was the sleeve of the shirt Adalyn had been wearing. He swallowed hard and moved closer, praying it wasn't covered in blood, but every one of his lawmen's instincts yelled for him to stop and take a closer look. Not at the sleeve but where he'd been about to step.

There, on the ground, he spotted the fist-size explosive device.

It would have no doubt blown him to smithereens had he stepped on it, and it made him wonder what other traps the killer had set.

Nolan kept moving, but he paid a lot more attention to where he was walking, and he kept his gun ready. With each step, he reminded himself he was getting closer and closer to Adalyn and that if the killer made it to her, Jeb and Cash would be able to stop another attempt to take her life.

Nolan made it to the back of the clearing, and he finally heard someone moving around. He zoomed in on the sound and spotted Adalyn. He didn't relax, not one bit, because they literally weren't out of these woods yet. Added to that, the killer might have escaped, which meant they might have to go through something like this all over again. At least this time though, there might be some DNA in the hazmat suit that could help them get an ID.

"It's me," Nolan risked whispering so that Cash and Jeb wouldn't turn their guns on him.

Adalyn's head whipped up, and her gaze homed in on him. Even in the darkness, he could see the relief along with the fresh cut on her head. She was bleeding, but she was alive.

Nolan started toward them but came to a dead stop when he heard another whisper.

"It's me," someone said in that same distorted voice.

That was the only warning Nolan got before he saw the hand snake out from the tree, and the shot tore through the woods. Not at him. No, the killer had a different target.

Adalyn.

ADALYN ONLY GOT a glimpse of the shooter before he fired. And it was a *he* all right. A man she recognized.

Cody.

Mercy, it was Cody.

That barely registered in her mind before she felt herself hit the ground. At first she thought she'd been shot. But no. Not her. Jeb. He'd pushed her down and had taken the bullet that had almost certainly been meant for her.

Clutching his shoulder, Jeb dropped down beside her, and all hell broke loose. She heard Nolan curse. Cash, too. And the gunshots started again. Loud, thick blasts that ripped through the trees. She prayed the bullets weren't ripping into Nolan and Cash.

Cody was a different matter.

She hoped he was dead. The man had caused so much misery and didn't deserve to live another second.

Beside her, Caroline was screaming now that she

was no longer gagged, and she was clutching on to Jeb. Cash, however, was focused on Cody, and that's where Adalyn put her focus, too. She took Jeb's gun, moved to the opposite side of the tree from Cash, and she tried to pinpoint Cody. She couldn't see him. He'd likely taken cover, but she could darn sure see Nolan.

Who wasn't behind cover.

He'd stepped out, taking aim at where she'd last seen Cody, and that made Nolan an easy target. Adalyn tried to do something about that.

"Still alive, Cody?" she called out.

One glimpse at Nolan, and she knew he hadn't seen the killer's face. He hadn't known that his own partner was the Grave Digger. She didn't want to think about how he was going to deal with that. For now, she just aimed both her attention, and the gun she was holding, in Cody's direction.

"I'm fine and dandy," Cody answered. He'd ditched the distorter so now she heard his familiar voice. And it turned her blood to ice.

Yes, they were dealing with a sociopath all right.

"Well, except for the little gunshot wound I arranged for myself," Cody went on. "FYI, getting shot hurts."

Too bad the hired gun hadn't missed and ended him then and there. Then, they wouldn't be going through this right now.

"I'm moving in on him," Adalyn whispered to Cash.

She could tell he wanted to argue, but she didn't wait

to hear it. Adalyn eased away from cover, and while keeping an eye on Nolan, she inched closer to Cody.

"How you doing, Nolan?" Cody asked, and she used the sound of his voice to locate his position.

Across from her Nolan was doing the same, but he was also glancing down at the ground as he walked. A reminder for her of the explosives Cody had used to attack them. There was no telling how much time he'd had in these woods to set up things. Hours. Because that's how long it'd been since Nolan and the marshals had moved Caroline and the others to the safe house. He could have come out ahead of them, dug the graves and waited until…

She mentally stopped, thinking of Russell.

Cody hadn't mentioned her former boss so maybe he was dead. Adalyn intended to find out though if he'd had a part in this or if he'd been just a pawn in Cody's sick game.

Adalyn moved closer, and when she spotted a dried twig in front of her, she purposely stepped on it, hoping it would make enough of a sound to draw Cody out. It did. He leaned out, automatically taking aim at her.

While Nolan took aim at him.

Nolan double tapped the trigger, and both shots slammed into Cody's chest.

Cody dropped, but Adalyn didn't let down her guard. Still watching where she was stepping, she hurried to him. Nolan did the same, and they came up on the killer at the same moment.

A killer who was clearly dying.

Cody hadn't been wearing Kevlar so there was blood all over the front of his shirt, but that didn't stop him from laughing. A laugh followed by a raspy cough, and he winced in pain.

Nolan went closer, and for just a moment his eyes met hers. Lots of things passed between them. Regret. Relief.

Love.

Well, there was plenty of love on her part anyway. Adalyn had no doubts as to how she felt about him. Later, she'd tell him, but for now, they had to deal with the man who'd made so many lives, including theirs, a living hell.

"You need an ambulance or the dead wagon?" Cash called out.

"Ambulance for now," Adalyn answered though she was pretty sure Cody would end up at the morgue. She couldn't feel one ounce of sympathy about that. "How's Jeb?"

"He'll be okay, but he'll be taking a trip to the hospital. I'll get that started."

Good. The sooner they were out of here, the better. But she wasn't leaving until she had answers. Apparently, Nolan felt the same way.

"Why?" Nolan asked Cody, and that one-word question held a lot of emotion. Including guilt. Something that Adalyn would assure him he shouldn't feel.

"Because I like it," Cody said, and he attempted another laugh. "It's fun. So is playing these games."

"This isn't a game," Nolan spit out.

"Beg to differ," Cody argued. "It became a game where I could recreate some history with my bitch of a mother. History where she dies, and I win."

So, Russell had been right about that. "Why not just go after your mother then?" Nolan wanted to know.

"Oh, I would have. I was saving her for last. And I would have had so much fun with her." When he smiled, there was blood on his mouth. "My mistake was hiring a henchman to help me this time with a few things. The explosives, nabbing Jeb in the house and setting up Jeremy. Hired help, big mistake."

"So, you killed all the other women on your own?" Adalyn asked.

"Oh, yeah. Different MOs, different personas. Being FBI gave me a good cover." He stopped, coughed and pressed his hand to his chest. The blood immediately began to seep through his fingers.

"You tried to set up Russell," Nolan pointed out.

"At first, I was going to set you up," Cody corrected. "Thought that'd be a new twist. So, I dug into your background and ran your DNA to find any secrets you might have. Found one when I learned Jeb Mercer, *the Law in Lubbock County*, was your daddy. I went from there to make this one fun game by kidnapping Caroline and bringing Jeb here so you two could meet. I figured bringing Jeb into the picture would mess with your head and you'd screw up the investigation."

Adalyn took a moment to process that. "So, Donny Ray, Russell, Jeremy or Gillian didn't help you?"

"No." Cody looked at her with mad, dying eyes. "I get all the credit. Just me."

She doubted that. Cody was lying because he wanted the sick "credit" for this nightmare. "I think you arranged for Jeremy to shoot you so you'd look innocent. Then, you killed him to silence him for good."

"Maybe," Cody admitted, but she could tell there was no *maybe* about it, that it was exactly what'd happened. "I put this all together."

"With Donny Ray's help?" Adalyn challenged.

"Hell, no." Cody was adamant this time. "He was just a little puzzle piece by kidnapping and selling Nolan all those years ago. He's nothing. Not like me. I'm something." His voice weakened, trailing off for a moment. "And you won simply because you got lucky."

She leaned in and let him see the fury in her eyes. "The only reason I was lucky is because Nolan shot, and stopped, you. Let that be the last thing you remember while you're dying. Nolan. Stopped. You."

Cody managed a lethal-looking glare before he mustered up another laugh. He looked at Nolan, not her. "You didn't stop me. I have one last surprise left. Set it up myself in case your *luck* led me to ending up here."

Adalyn froze. And prayed he was bluffing.

"Your backup should be at your house now," Cody said. "Russell, too, since I left him tied up in one of the barns. And at least some of them are gonna die," he added with the last breath he'd ever take. "You lose. I win."

That's when Adalyn heard the explosion.

Chapter Sixteen

Nolan didn't have to guess where the explosion had happened. He knew Cody hadn't used his dying breath to lie. Of course, there'd obviously been plenty of other lies and untruths that Cody had told that would haunt Nolan for the rest of his life. But this had been the truth.

And that meant Cody could add more deaths to his already deadly toll.

Later, Nolan would find out exactly how many people his partner had killed, but for now he had to get back to the ranch house and see if he could help. That included taking Jeb back with him so he could get to the hospital.

"I owe you," Nolan told Jeb, and he helped Cash get the man to his feet. "For saving Adalyn."

"You don't owe me anything," Jeb assured him.

Nolan heard the unspoken *son* that Jeb had added to the tail end of that. It didn't set Nolan's teeth on edge, didn't make him think of being taken away from a father who'd apparently loved him.

No, it made him feel, well, settled.

A shocker considering they were all scraped up and beat to hell. But there was a bottom line here, and it was the Grave Digger was dead and they were alive. Unfortunately, he couldn't say the same for anyone who happened to be back at the ranch.

"You need me to stay behind and secure the scene and Cody's body?" Adalyn asked him, drawing Nolan's attention. Not that his attention had strayed too far from her.

"No, I want you with me." And that was a truth that included a lot more than the next few minutes.

"You think there are any other hired guns around?" Adalyn pressed.

"No." That wasn't just lip service, either, to get some of that worry off her face.

If Cody had had another hired gun, he would have taunted them with that before he died. Or used whatever henchman was available to try to get him out of there. Still, Nolan kept watch just in case he was wrong.

Caroline was crying when Nolan managed to get her into the SUV. Some of the tears were for worry over Jeb, but he thought a few of them were of the happy, relieved variety. Hard not to be relieved when you were still breathing, and the man who'd made your life a living hell wasn't.

They all got into the SUV, and Nolan sped away, just as he'd done on the frantic, heart-stopping drive to get to Adalyn. Everything in him had focused on saving Caroline and her. Now, he had to see if there was anyone he could save from Cody's last-ditch stand.

"I'll call for a bomb squad and more EMTs," Cash offered from the back seat.

For just a second, Nolan met the man's eyes in the rearview mirror, silently thanking him. Not just for the calls he was already making but because Cash had been there tonight. For Adalyn, Caroline and Jeb. But also for him.

"The bleeding's slowed down," Jeb relayed while Cash made the call. He was between Caroline and Cash, and Caroline was applying pressure to the wound. "Hurts like hell, but I'm not going to bleed out."

Nolan was extremely thankful for that. Not just because he wanted Jeb to live and make a full recovery, but also because he didn't want Adalyn having to live with the guilt over Jeb having taken a bullet for her.

Even though that's exactly what Jeb had done.

Cody might not have killed Adalyn with that shot, but he damn sure would have tried to end her life then and there. That would be the stuff of more nightmares for Nolan. For Adalyn, too. Heck, for all of them.

Before the house even came into view, Nolan spotted the smoke rising up into the night sky. There were also sirens blaring. Backup vehicles, no doubt.

He steeled himself up and kept speeding toward the scene. And it was a scene all right. The house was on fire. Not a small, containable blaze, either. The orangey red flames were already jutting up through the roof.

Cash cursed. "Cody had his hired henchman use a whole lot of explosives here."

Yeah, he had, and if anyone had been inside, they were almost certainly dead.

Nolan braked to a stop a good twenty yards from the house, and along with his gun, he dragged out his badge so he could identify himself and wouldn't get hit with friendly fire.

"I'm Special Agent Nolan Dalton," he called out to anyone who could hear him.

It turned out to be a lot of anyones. When he rounded the side of the house, he saw the two cruisers from the local sheriff's office, and there were four deputies in the front yard. Some were on the phone. Others were firing glances all around as if looking for the culprit who'd done this.

"Nolan," one of the deputies greeted him. Sam Cordova. One of Nolan's old high school friends.

"Are there any deputies inside the house?" Nolan asked, and he clipped his badge to his belt to free up his hand.

Sam shook his head, and Nolan felt some of the tension ease up in his gut. It was a miracle that Cody hadn't succeeded in adding to his death toll.

The deputy's gaze slid to Jeb, who was being bolstered up by both Caroline and Cash, and he hurried over to help. "What happened here?" Sam asked Nolan as he helped ease Jeb to a sitting position on the ground.

Nolan dragged in a long breath and decided to give him the condensed version for now. "The Grave Digger's responsible. He's dead in the woods," he added when Sam's shoulders snapped back. "His hired gun is dead in there." He tipped his head to the house just as the roof collapsed.

"Good," Sam muttered. "You okay?"

Nolan figured *to be determined* would sound way too flip. And he wasn't. He was thankful, worried and more than a little sick that he hadn't seen what was in Cody and stopped him.

"There's a man tied up in one of the barns," Nolan told Sam. "His name's Russell Mason. He'll probably need medical attention. But watch for any other explosives. I don't think there are any more or they would have gone off the same time as the one in the house, but just be careful."

Sam nodded and shouted out to one of his fellow deputies that they needed to check the barns. "The ambulance and the fire department should be here any minute now," Sam added as he hurried off to start the search for Russell.

Nolan made a quick check on Jeb and saw the bleeding had indeed slowed. Jeb was clearly in pain, but he wasn't dying. Then, Nolan allowed himself to look at Adalyn. Really look at her. He'd avoided doing that in the woods and in the SUV because he hadn't wanted to risk losing focus until he was sure they were safe.

He lost that focus now by taking hold of her chin and turning her face to the side so he could examine her for any injuries. There were some fresh cuts, including the one on her forehead that might need a couple of stitches.

"I'm okay," she assured him. Nolan lost a whole lot more focus when she put her arms around him and pulled her to him. "We're both okay."

Again, he wasn't going with a *to be determined* response because he knew she was right. They were alive and the Grave Digger was dead. That didn't fix all their problems, but it sure as heck took care of the biggest ones.

Another of those problems got his attention when the rest of the roof caved in. He could hear the sirens from a fire engine in the distance, but it wouldn't get there in time to save any part of the house.

"I'm sorry," Adalyn murmured as she followed his gaze. "You lost your family home."

"It's all right. I'd already lost it," Nolan whispered back.

That loss had happened when Donny Ray had gunned down his father. Now, it was just a burning house, and once it'd been taken down to ashes, he could decide if he wanted to rebuild. Of course, he'd lost all the things inside, but his family hadn't been that sentimental about keeping things. Besides, he had what was important right here in his arms.

The fire engine came to a stop in front of what was left of the house, and not one but two ambulances were right behind them. Nolan called out to the first set of EMTs who exited their vehicle so they would head straight to Jeb. Keeping his arm around Adalyn, Nolan went to him.

Not sure what to say to the man who'd fathered

him, and lost him for so many years, Nolan just settled for another "Thank you."

Jeb nodded and kept his gaze pinned to Nolan's
even while the EMTs started to examine him. "Maybe
when I'm fixed up, we can talk," Jeb said.

"We will," Nolan assured him. "Let me make sure
things are tied up here, and then we'll head to the
hospital." Where he fully intended to have a doctor
examine Adalyn.

"I'm going with Jeb in the ambulance," Caroline
insisted.

"If there's room, so will I," Cash added.

"There's room," one of the EMTs assured him.

Cash looked at Nolan then and extended his hand
for him to shake. Nolan accepted it, silently offering a
truce to his brother. This wasn't a time for a family reunion and baring one's soul, but it was a start. A darn
good one. Apparently, he'd come from a blue blood
family, and that was something he could live with.

"You're still the kid brother," Cash added, giving Nolan a light jab on the arm. "A kid brother to
Leigh, too, which puts you way down low in the peck-
ing order."

Nolan didn't bother to stop the smile from form-
ing on his mouth. This wasn't exactly a smiling moment, but again, it was a start.

After the EMTs had loaded Jeb onto a stretcher,
Adalyn leaned down and gave the man a quick hug.
A hug that caused Jeb's eyes to water a little.

"We'll see you soon at the hospital," she murmured

to him, and when she turned, she got more hugs. First from Caroline and then from Cash.

"Do something to make sure that cut on Adalyn's head gets tended to," Cash added to Nolan, and after giving him another arm jab, he followed Jeb, Caroline and the EMTs to the ambulance.

Nolan just stood there, watching them go, and then he turned to Adalyn. She was smiling a little now, too. "We're all going to be okay," she assured him.

Yeah, they were. There'd be bumps, of course, but he'd take those. Nolan was about to tell her just that when he heard Sam call out.

"We found Russell Mason," the deputy shouted from the side driveway that led to the barns. "I think he's okay, but I want him checked out." He motioned for one of the EMTs to follow him to the barn.

Good. That was another of those loose ends tied up. As soon as the ERT arrived, that'd tie up some things as well because it would mean he could turn over everything to them, including Cody's body. Then, he could get Adalyn the heck out of there.

"I'll owe Russell an apology for thinking he was the Grave Digger," Nolan said. "And for not believing him when he pointed the finger at Cody." He'd owe Gillian one, too, but the one to her wouldn't exactly be heartfelt since she had conspired with Donny Ray to stalk Adalyn.

Adalyn made a sound of agreement. "I'll apologize, too, but I'm not going back to my job. I'm thinking about getting my badge back. You know, like a fresh start."

Nolan smiled again. "I'm all for fresh starts. And renewing some not so fresh. I want you with me, Adalyn."

He kissed her to remind her of exactly what that entailed and because he needed to have the taste of her in his mouth. Heck, he needed everything about her. With the fire snapping behind them and the heavy smell of smoke swirling around, he gathered her close and looked into her eyes.

"Are you going to tell me you love me and you don't want to live without me?" she came out and asked.

Nolan froze and studied her expression, trying to figure out if she had any objections to that. Her smile let him know that she didn't. Good. Because he wanted no objections, no doubts.

"Yes," he confirmed. "I was about to say exactly that."

"Good. Then, I'll say it first. I'm in love with you, and I don't want to live without you. I want you in my arms and in my bed. Or yours." Adalyn chuckled. "I'm flexible on that."

Mercy, it felt good to hear her laugh. It felt even better when he pulled her to him and sank right into the kiss she offered him. Nolan didn't wait even a second longer to get started on that new fresh start.

* * * * *

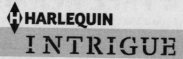

Get 4 FREE REWARDS!

We'll send you 2 FREE Books plus <u>2 FREE Mystery Gifts</u>.

FREE Value Over **$20**

Both the **Harlequin Intrigue**® and **Harlequin**® **Romantic Suspense** series feature compelling novels filled with heart-racing action-packed romance that will keep you on the edge of your seat.

HARLEQUIN
PLUS

Try the best multimedia
subscription service for romance
readers like you!

Read, Watch and Play.

Experience the easiest way to get
the romance content you crave.

Start your **FREE TRIAL** at
<u>www.harlequinplus.com/freetrial</u>.